MURDER IN HAWAII

MURDER IN HAWAII

Dorothy Brenner Francis

Thorndike Press • Chivers Press
Waterville, Maine USA   Bath, England

This Large Print edition is published by Thorndike Press, USA and by Chivers Press, England.

Published in 2002 in the U.S. by arrangement with Maureen Moran Agency.

Published in 2002 in the U.K. by arrangement with the author.

U.S. Hardcover 0-7862-4530-1 (Romance Series)
U.K. Hardcover 0-7540-7429-3 (Chivers Large Print)
U.K. Softcover 0-7540-7430-7 (Camden Large Print)

The text of this Large Print edition is unabridged.
Other aspects of the book may vary from the original edition.

Cover design by Deirdre Wait.

Set in 16 pt. Plantin by Rick Gundberg.

Printed in the United States on permanent paper.

British Library Cataloguing in Publication Data available

Library of Congress Control Number: 2002107271
ISBN 0-7862-4530-1

To my agent, Ruth Cantor.

CHAPTER ONE

As the plane stopped on the Lihue airstrip, I forced to my lips the self-confident smile I had practiced for so many years. It hid the fears that left me shattered and bewildered. I clutched my purse as if ready to produce the worn letter, should anyone question my right to be here. How silly! No one was apt to challenge me, least of all the pretty Oriental stewardess in her hibiscus-flowered holomuu.

By choice I was the last one off the plane, and I paused momentarily on the exit ramp. An emerald border of lush tropical growth rimmed the airstrip, and the Hawaiian sky fanned into a smooth backdrop for the clouds floating by. But in the background, cloud-shrouded mountains stood like specters threatening to smother the sun-filled day. The trade wind ruffled my hair as I ducked down the steps from plane to ground and headed toward the baggage claim area.

Diesel exhaust tainted the air, and the jet engines' whine blotted out lesser sounds. I watched two dark-skinned natives hoist mounds of luggage from the plane, pile it on a cart, and wheel it across the airstrip.

I was pressing toward my two light-blue cases when a short, withered leaf of a man wearing a flat-crowned, palm-frond hat and faded work denims darted from nowhere. He swooped up my bags and melted into the crowd.

"Stop!" I called. "Wait! You've made a mistake!"

Tourists turned to watch, and a friendly baggage boy rushed to my aid.

"Trouble, Miss?" His teeth gleamed like white coral in the brown crescent of his smile.

"That man!" I stabbed the air in the direction of the small figure skinning through the crowd toward the entrance of the terminal building. "He's stolen my suitcases."

"You are sure, Miss? Perhaps you've made an error. Many bags — dey have twins."

I shook my head. "Hurry!"

The Hawaiian dashed off, and by the time I reached the terminal entrance he was returning with a small dark man who cocked one black eyebrow and gazed up at me in utter disdain.

"Perhaps you are Miss Virginia Ardan?" the baggage boy asked.

"Why, yes. Yes, I am." A mixture of surprise and uneasiness washed over me, and I struggled to keep my face from betraying my alarm. How had these strangers learned my name?

"Dis is your driver, Davao Thal, from Hale Malani!"

"Oh! I'm so sorry!" I felt my face flush as Davao Thal studied me with owllike, unwinking eyes.

"Please forgive me, Mr. Thal. I had no idea . . ." My voice faded as I dug into my purse for change to tip the baggage boy, then I followed Davao Thal to a sleek black car.

My first impression of this man had been wrong. Although well past middle years, he was more weathered than withered. The ropy muscles in his tanned arms and the deeply grooved furrows in his umber-colored face bespoke a lifetime spent working out-of-doors.

After formally ushering me into the car's rear seat, Mr. Thal again dissolved into the crowd, and I leaned back as I sat watching the throng. I felt uneasy, exposed. Why had my sister's driver snatched my luggage so quickly? I carried nothing of special interest. Again I was letting Delores' letter unnerve me. Delores had undoubtedly told her man how to recognize both me and my luggage, and he had just happened to see the bags first.

I suppose I should have been expecting someone to meet me; Delores had written that she hadn't left the villa since Blaine's funeral. I had not expected her to come to Lihue. I had assumed that I would take a taxi to the House of Malani.

Hale Malani. "Hall-lay." I murmured the word, trying for the baggage boy's fluid accent. Then I stopped, afraid that Davao Thal would appear and find me talking to myself.

All around me a holiday mood prevailed. I heard the sensuous strum of a guitar, and mellow-smooth voices sang island songs from a palm-shaded terrace while friends greeted each other with kisses and flower leis.

Ever since Delores had married and moved to Hawaii two years ago, I had read every book and article about the islands that I could find. Now that I was actually on Kauai, I had the strange sensation that I was returning home rather than running away to hide in a strange land.

It only seemed natural that the tall Hawaiian wearing a brown straw hat banded with a shocking-pink feather lei should drape a necklace of lavender blossoms on the shoulders of an Oriental woman, kiss her soundly, then escort her to a candy-striped rental jeep. Even the jasmine fragrance which perfumed the air seemed familiar as did the exotic costumes of the people. I was unsurprised at the ankle-length dresses which spangled bits of paintbox color into the August afternoon, or at the flowing muumuus or the Japanese happi coats.

Leaning forward in the car, I noticed one beautiful girl wearing a softly folded sari of India, while my own travel suit exuded all the charm of a burlap negligee.

Only a few minutes passed before Davao Thal returned. As he reached the car, a black haze masked the sun, and rain spattered the windshield. This storm was unlike pelting Iowa rains. It was as if a miasma of evil had suddenly enveloped us. I shuddered as Davao drove along a deserted stretch of countryside. Then the rain stopped as suddenly as it had started, and bright sunshine turned the cane fields into squares of shimmering green.

Davao Thal ignored me. I wondered if he could be one of the "they" that Delores mentioned in her letter — one of those who "refused to listen."

Mr. Thal remained silent, but I couldn't blame him for being miffed at me for thinking him a thief, so I leaned forward to make amends.

"It is forgotten, Miss Ardan." Davao's stringent voice twanged like a flat cello string, and I realized that these were the first words I had heard him utter.

"How far do we have to drive, Davao?"

"Many miles, Miss."

Although Davao Thal seemed sworn to silence, I tried once more. "I've read so much about this garden isle that I can hardly wait to see it all — Waimea Canyon, Mount Waialeale, the Haena caves."

"Mount Waialeale rises to your right," Davao said. "Perhaps you'll see all you want of Kauai in a very few days."

In the rearview mirror I watched Davao's left brow lift toward his hairline, and I had the uneasy feeling that he hoped my visit would indeed be brief. I made no more attempt at conversation as I gazed at the veil of black clouds and gray misty rain which shrouded the tall peak of Mount Waialeale.

Delores had mentioned that Hale Malani was "quite a distance" from the airport, so I turned from the somber mountain and gazed toward the sun-flecked ocean where coconut palms bent into the breeze. I settled back to enjoy the drive, determined to ignore Davao's dour presence.

Although I knew from experience how much Delores hated asking for help, my own need for sanctuary diminished her troubles in my eyes. Surely her foreboding of danger was derived from Blaine's death, from the cutting pain of grief and despair.

I was ready to forget about New York and Matt Jackson and singing and practicing and auditions and recording sessions and waiting and waiting and waiting. All that was past. Now a whole glorious future of sunshine and white sand beaches beckoned. I tried to ease my mind in this pleasant lazy future of my dreams, but Delores' letter intruded. The realization that she desperately needed help had nagged at me; I had almost worn the pale gray sheet to tatters rereading the letter, trying to puzzle out its meaning. Even now I could see the words. The message was etched on my brain.

Dear Ginny,

Forget New York. I've found a job for you here. Please come. You must. Blaine was no fool, but they won't listen when I tell them. Even Ward has turned against me. There's much I need to understand, but the danger, the evil that lurks on this island, perhaps in Hale Malani itself, is real and I am frightened. How soon may I expect you?

Love,
Delores

I repeated the terse message to myself and

felt a growing sense of unrest as I stared blindly through the car window. So Delores had found work for me. That was the least of my worries. Any twenty-four-year-old college graduate should be able to find some sort of employment. Yet the promise of a job gave my visit an aura of permanence that pleased me more than I cared to admit. My real concern was over the rest of the letter.

What was behind those guarded words? I knew that Ward Malani was Blaine's older brother, a sort of family black sheep, but who were the others, the "they" to whom Delores referred?

For years my sister had seemed stubbornly bent on proving that she could manage on her own. That's the thing that made her cry for help all the more troubling. As young children we had never been close; I had loved to hike and swim, while Delores had preferred to read or play with dolls. The four-year difference in our ages had yawned like a chasm between us, but disaster has a way of strengthening all bonds.

Divorce affects children in various ways. It marked me with an agonizing sense of inadequacy, an ever-growing conviction that if I had been a more worthwhile person my parents would have stayed together, would have protected the family unit at all costs.

14

Delores was ten and I was fourteen when Father ran away with another woman, an artist of some fame whose lecture tour through the Midwest had ended in a prolonged visit with relatives in our small Iowa town. Mom, Delores, and I were left to face the divorce and a maelstrom of small-town gossip.

At first my inferiority feelings were vague, but gradually they mushroomed into dread and agony until my fear of being exposed as an unworthy person bordered on phobia. I even began having a recurring dream in which I stood alone, spotlighted on a huge stage. In the dream I could not see my audience, but I could hear their derisive laughter, hear it until I awakened in a cold sweat.

Although lacerated in spirit, Mom went back to teaching high school English to help support us. As the years passed, Delores concentrated on making friends, on doing her utmost to develop a personality that drew people to her, while I worked at hiding my true self, my worthless inner being, from the prying eyes of the world. I felt that I had to prove myself worthy. I lived with a compulsion to conquer all obstacles in my path, and I developed a hardheaded habit of always tackling the most difficult tasks first.

Because of our broken home, and because Mom seemed frail and weary, I gave up plans to study music at Oberlin College. I enrolled at the state university so I could be home on weekends and keep a protective eye on my family. My choice was also a good cover-up for not dating. Although I protested, I gradually became the honored guest on my visits.

I think now that Delores was always the strong one. By the time she was a senior in high school, she managed the house for Mom and at the same time kept up with her studies and an active social life. And she worried about me.

"Ginny, it's unfair," Delores said one snowy Friday night after Mom had retired and we were alone sipping hot chocolate in the warm glow from the living room fireplace. "You never have any fun! You needn't come home every weekend, you know. I feel terrible about your missing all the college parties and ball games."

"Would you believe that I like it here? You're a great help to Mom, but I always feel better after I've been home to see that everything's okay. Anyway, I'm not swamped with invitations."

Even then I hated to admit that my homing pigeon act was a ruse to avoid meeting and dating boys. I told myself that I had no intention of becoming ensnared in the same trap that caught Mom — marriage — but that was a lie. I was afraid — afraid to form any intimate friendships that might expose my inadequacies as a person. It was easier to leave campus on weekends than to devise reasons for avoiding dates. But Dee wasn't fooled.

"You could have scads of dates if you'd just, well . . . You could change if you wanted to, Ginny. That red hair! Those blue eyes! Fire and ice! As far as looks go, you're a knockout."

"Dee! You know dates bore me."

"But they shouldn't, Ginny. You're hiding, hiding behind a domino wall. One good jolt would start a chain reaction that would bring it down to where you could at least step over the debris. I think it's time you stopped being hurt by a marriage that flopped." Delores broke off, aware that she had said too much.

I wanted to change. I really did. But there is a big difference in wanting to and in being able to. All my iron-jawed willpower failed.

I gazed at the crackling mulberry logs without answering. Like Mom, Delores was a natural beauty with auburn hair, sea-green eyes, and a face that needed no makeup. But I took after Father. I was big-boned, tall, and as muscular as an athlete, and I hated my crop of carroty-orange hair. I held few illusions; I never imagined myself anything but plain. My one salvation was my clear soprano voice;

singing came to me as naturally as breathing. Big girl: big tone.

Although I was determined in my pursuit of a singing career, I knew that Delores was right, that I was hiding from the core of life. Nobody guessed my secret; society makes it easy for people like me to rationalize their actions.

When Delores asked me to come to Kauai, my roommate, a fashion designer, not only volunteered to store my few possessions and take over our apartment, but she also made me a green silk after-swim turban as a going-away gift. She believed that I was unselfishly abandoning my career in order to help my sister. But I knew the truth. I would do anything for Delores, but deep down I knew I was still trying to hide my inadequacies from the world.

Mom died soon after Delores was graduated from high school. Her death saddened us, and although we were closer than ever before, Delores utterly startled me with her decision to leave Iowa.

"I'm going to New York with you." Delores spoke with decision and authority, and I knew I would never be able to change her mind. Still, I tried.

"But, Dee, Mom counted on your going to college. Enroll at Iowa City. You can visit me during vacations."

"I won't bother you in New York, Ginny. College just isn't for me. Anyway, I want to see Dad; I think he owes me a welcome, don't you?"

My stomach knotted. In my estimation a list of the things that our father owed us would fill a book. But we seldom mentioned his name, and I was nonplussed at the idea of Delores even thinking of seeing him again after all these years.

"I don't know why," Delores said, "but I want to know what he's really like. Maybe everyone's misjudged him. You'll let me tag along, won't you?"

Delores went to New York. I had planned to take private vocal lessons from Professor Matthew Jackson, to find part-time work doing anything that resulted in a paycheck, and to search for a singing job. For the first time since my parents' divorce I felt a touch of self-confidence. Nobody in New York knew me. Maybe I could hide my personal deficiencies behind my voice.

Father was listed in the phone directory. Delores elected to pay him a surprise visit, and as that was the last I saw of her for several weeks, I assumed that she had made some sort of peace with him. She always phoned me on Saturday, but her conversations were terse and stilted as if she feared someone might be eavesdropping.

My life was busy, and I was one of the lucky ones. A soprano in the chorus of an off-Broadway musical, *Jingle Jolly*, decided to leave the show, and Professor Jackson arranged an audition for me. By some wink of fate I landed the job. This was the New York of my dreams; I was an employed musician sure that spiraling success waited in the near future. Lessons, private practice, and chorus rehearsals filled my life; there was no time for parties or dates, and I was glad. Who could blame a girl for giving up her social life for so glamorous a career?

I was busier than ever before and I would have enjoyed every moment of every day if inner voices hadn't begun to shout that I was only half a person, that a career wasn't everything, and that I was dodging the very heart of life.

Now, driving along the Hawaiian countryside, a million questions filled my mind, but pride prevented me from voicing any to Davao Thal.

The black asphalt road hugged the white shoreline most of the way, and the palm-fringed beaches were deserted. Here and there fishing boats or pleasure crafts dotted the water.

Suddenly Davao braked the car in the middle of the road and stared out across the Pacific. I followed his gaze over a gnarled tangle of cereus vines, through a frame of fringed Pandanus leaves, and finally out to the sea where the light-green water along the beach gave way to a deeper shade of blue that bespoke great depth.

"It happened here. Pindora found his body on this beach at low tide. Right there; face down in the sand." Davao stared a bit longer, meshed the gears, and drove on down the road. He might have been speaking to me, but I had the eerie feeling that he was talking to himself, and I knew without asking that he referred to Blaine Malani. His words chilled me. Although the day was warm, I shivered as the road veered away from the beach and we turned onto a narrow lane over which an arched signboard read HALE MALANI.

CHAPTER TWO

Gaunt Norfolk pines studded either side of the driveway, forming a spikelike fence which restrained the voluptuous growth of a hibiscus hedge whose blood-red blossoms writhed in the wind as we drove past. As the car swayed on a rising curve, I saw the rectangular brown house which dominated the hillside. Only when Davao drove into the carport did I fully perceive Hale Malani's mansionlike proportions.

A pagoda-type roof overspread the two-story structure and shaded the planked balcony which rimmed the house at the second story level. Tall sliding-glass doors both upstairs and down were like monster eyes staring from the pitted-stone walls. Announcing that some manner of construction was underway, a carpenter's scaffolding stood under the wrought-iron balcony railing on the side of the house away from the sea.

Without waiting for Davao's aid, I stepped from the car onto the flagged terrace. Pausing to inhale the cloying odor of tropical blossoms, I heard the wind hiss through the giant philodendrons which twined around the two Golden Shower trees on either side of the front entryway and then snaked along the railing of the redwood balcony.

In the waiting silence I tried to shake the gloom that gripped me. What was there about this villa that made me reluctant to enter? I saw a certain beauty in the fall of yellow blossoms from the Golden Showers, and the tip-tilt corners of the Oriental roof lent the house a rakish air. But the somber brown rock chilled me, and the philodendron's lush greenery seemed obscene in its flamboyance.

Davao Thal hurried inside carrying my bags, and in a moment I heard the muted swish of woven sandals against flagstones as Delores rushed to greet me with a fragrant lei and a kiss.

"Aloha, Ginny!" She looked up at me with a bright smile. "It's great to see you! I thought you'd never arrive. Let's relax on the lanai for a few minutes. Pindora's on her way with some cold drinks. How was your trip?"

I followed Delores to the side terrace which overlooked the ocean. With a wry thought for the way my carroty hair would clash with the scarlet blaze of cushions, I sank into an inviting bamboo chair.

"Let me catch my breath!" I laughed and tried to relax. Although I had been looking forward to seeing my sister again, the thought of her recent bereavement made me edgy; I was afraid of saying the wrong thing.

When Delores sat down, I realized how completely worn-out she looked. The undeniable beauty was still there, but her dark dress sapped the color from her cheeks, and her auburn hair seemed dry and brittle where it fanned across the green cushion of her chair. Her first whirlwind surge of animation must only have been keyed-up excitement at my arrival, for the sea-colored eyes which once flashed like emeralds now had the opaque look of turquoise, and when she stopped chewing her lower lip long enough to smile, it was the sad sweet smile of a nostalgic dreamer. How different Delores was. How changed. As we sat there I remembered her vitality, her sparkling enthusiasm the day she called to tell me of her engagement to Blaine.

"Ginny!" Her voice bubbled like champagne. "I'm being married! Next week! Say you'll be my maid of honor. I want you with me, I want you to meet Blaine; I know you'll love him too. Ginny! Ginny, are you there?"

"Delores!" I could hardly speak let alone find words to answer her. My mind shouted. No. You're too young. Who is he? Wait!

Where did you meet? Wait! But all I could say was, "Delores!"

Interpreting my speechlessness as approval, Delores babbled on like the teenager she was. I pieced together the information that Father was sponsoring the small wedding at his apartment, that the groom was one Blaine Malani from Kauai, Hawaii, and that Delores had met him three weeks ago at a Yale University dance. Of course I promised to be in the wedding party and I began practicing my expression, the smile that masked my inner agonies.

I dreaded meeting Father, but I need not have worried. He skipped the wedding rehearsal, and the following morning after our first awkward greeting, I saw little more of him. It was as if he were a stranger, and I made no attempt to become acquainted. Our meeting hadn't hurt. This wasn't the father I remembered; I could hardly associate this sleek, sophisticated creature with the carefree person who once had shared my life in Iowa. But a wedding is a happy occasion, and I tried not to do or say anything that might leave unpleasant memories for Delores.

In a milieu of lavish surroundings my sister managed to keep her wedding simple, and in spite of all my misgivings I was happy for her. Blaine Malani, who she explained was Hawaiian-Chinese-Caucasian, was a handsome, well-educated young man who was preparing to manage a family island-resort hotel. He obviously adored Delores, and I swept all my unspoken reasons as to why the marriage might fail into a crevice of my mind.

But as usual where my sister was concerned, my worries were unfounded. Delores had written to me regularly over the last two years, and the wire containing the news of Blaine's accidental death was the only message that carried any emotion other than blissful happiness. Illness prevented me from attending the funeral, but nothing could have held me in New York after I received Delores' last letter.

Bamboo furniture cushioned in tones of scarlet, green, and gold accented the lanai, this open porch on which we were sitting, and the potted orchids and anthuriums splashed a rainbow of hues onto the scene. It was hard to believe that anything but gaiety could survive here; yet Delores' sad expression and smoke-colored sheath stood out like a somber thread in a brightly colored tapestry.

"It's wonderful to be here, Dee," I said before I lied a little, "and you're looking great." I inhaled the jasmine scent that drifted from the creamy white lei around my neck. "Mm, what are these?"

"Pikake. Like them?"

"They're heavenly," I said.

"To give you a really proper welcome I should have let Davao present the lei to you at the airport, but somehow I just couldn't picture his doing it with a true aloha spirit."

I smiled. "That I can understand."

"He met you promptly, didn't he?" Delores frowned. "I never know what to expect from Davao now that Blaine's gone."

"Don't worry on my account," I said. "He acted with great efficiency. In fact, he claimed my bags so quickly that I thought he was a thief trying to steal them. I'm afraid I made a bit of a scene at the airport. Later I realized that you must have described my luggage to him, but I still can't understand why he was much more interested in the luggage than in me."

"Glad to hear you say that." Delores' face sobered. "Ever since Blaine's death, I've felt that Davao has some personal dislike for me, but his wife, Pindora, says he hasn't. She says that he considers women his inferiors. Your experience certainly upholds her point. He has many ways of flaunting his superiority."

"Must you put up with that? Must you keep him?"

"I hate to let him go," Delores said. "He's been with Blaine's family since he was a young man. It seems unfair to cashier him now; he still does his work well as long as his orders don't come from me. Ward's presence solves most of *that* problem. Do tell me about your trip."

Delores' emphasis on the word *that* indicated other problems, but whether they dealt with Davao or Blaine's brother Ward I couldn't guess. I hadn't known that Ward was living at the villa, and for some reason I found the news disturbing. But I flashed Delores my special cover-up smile. As I began a brief narrative about my journey, a small butterfly of a woman fluttered onto the terrace bearing our drinks. The bell skirt of her saffron-colored dress danced in the breeze as she served us.

"Ginny, this is Pindora Thal, Davao's wife."

I smiled into the pretty face where two merry eyes gleamed like jet marbles from beneath a fringe of ebony hair.

"Hello, Pindora, I'm glad to know you. The drinks are delicious."

"Thank you, Missy." Pindora's voice was butter-soft and blurred with accent. She smiled pleasantly, her actions in definite contrast to her husband's. Clearly, Pindora desired to please, but she darted away before I could say more, her sandals whispering over the flagged stones.

I hated to approach the subject of Blaine's death, but I had postponed the unpleasant task as long as I could, and anyway I thought it was time that Delores explained her strange letter.

"I'm sorry I couldn't come for the funeral," I said. "It must have been absolutely ghastly for you, but the doctor made me sign in blood that I'd stay in bed with that case of mumps. Mumps! Of all things."

"I wish you could have come." Delores gazed at the undulating ocean. "But you're here now, and that's even nicer. I've been lonely."

"How did it happen? The accident, I mean?"

"Nobody really knows." Delores lolled her head against a soft cushion. "Blaine took the outboard out fishing late in the afternoon. He never returned. I never saw him again until Pindora . . ."

"I know. Davao told me. There was a storm?"

"Oh, the ocean was a bit choppy, and the surf was up, but Blaine knew how to handle that boat. He was raised in these islands. He tangled with something besides a rough sea." Dee leaned forward and her eyes flashed sparks of the old fire that I remembered.

"Dee! Do you suspect murder?"

"I'm confused." Delores sighed, and as she sipped her drink a languid shrug of her shoulders smothered her brief spark of agitation. "But I know that Blaine was an expert seaman and swimmer and that he had enough gumption to know when the ocean was too rough for him. The investigators called his death accidental — said he drowned following a severe blow on the head."

"What about his boat?" I kept prodding, probing, hoping Delores would speak of the letter on her own accord.

"That's a mystery. Blaine's body washed ashore a few miles from here, but no trace of the *Golden Dolphin* has been found. Ward discovered a few yellow-painted boards in a nearby cove, but they turned out to be fragments from an old PT boat which some men had tried unsuccessfully to convert into a pleasure craft. The *Golden Dolphin* hasn't turned up."

I pulled the gray sheet from my purse. "Tell me what's bothering you. Perhaps I can help."

In a flash Delores snatched the message from me, tore it into shreds, and thrust them into her pocket. "I hoped you'd forget that silly letter, Ginny. I was terribly upset when I wrote it, and even if there's truth in my suspicions I'll have to find it myself."

Delores left me openmouthed, yet this was the girl I remembered. Impulsive as a March wind Delores always had given the impression of leaping before she looked, but somehow her jumps were generally in the right direction. Mom and I had viewed her headstrongness as admirable determination. At least she still had this old spark.

Delores rose and stood before me unconsciously stiffening her knees as if bracing herself against a hostile world. "Oh, I still want you, need you here with me. You can't imagine how much better I feel now that I've seen you again. You'll help me forget the accident; I want to remember Blaine as he was — happy, healthy, and very much in love with me. Sometimes I can almost sense his footstep on the stairs and hear him call my name."

My curiosity about Delores' letter was unsatisfied, but all my sympathy went out to her as I saw her struggling to accept the largest "no" of her life — no Blaine. As soon as we finished our drinks, she led the way into the house.

"The outdoor lanai-terrace is our main living room," Delores said. "We use this indoor family room only when it rains or on the few nights when it's chilly. On your right is a more formal drawing room that we seldom enter."

Delores straightened a gilt-framed portrait

on the foyer wall, then paused before a large mirror that hung at the bottom of the stairway which spiraled like a corkscrew toward the second floor. I looked around, trying to see everything at once. Although gayly decorated, the interior of the villa was somehow as forbidding as the exterior, but this central hallway with its winding staircase and arched doorways revealed an atmosphere of casual elegance.

The family room glowed with color. Tapaprint draperies floated at the sides of the sliding doors, bright-hued pillows confettied the bamboo furniture, and burnished brass lanterns swung from the rustic, beamed ceiling. Only the utilitarian scaffolding visible through the wide panels of plate glass detracted from the scene.

"Carpenter's day off?" I nodded toward the platform outside.

Delores followed me to the window. "Oh, some men from the village are supposed to come this week or next to examine a section of the balcony. Termites are a real problem here in the islands, and Ward suspects that some of those timbers may be honeycombed with rot. Between Ward and the carpenters you'll surely be in for some noise while you're here."

Again I heard disparagement in Delores'

voice as she mentioned her brother-in-law, but she drew me back toward the foyer, and I was too engrossed in admiring the drawing room to ask questions.

This elegant sitting room was richly formal, and I stepped far enough inside the archway to feel the spring of the ivory-colored carpeting and to touch the creamy satin brocade of the divan. A green Japanese silk screen blocked off a rear doorway, and in front of it, on a carved koa-wood table, an arrangement of yellow plumeria blossoms lent their gentle incense to point up the Oriental decor.

"Pindora and Davao have the rooms at the back of the villa across from the kitchen," Delores said. "Come on up and see the second floor."

I followed Delores up the graceful curve of steps to where six bedrooms opened off the balustraded hallway surrounding the staircase. She stepped inside one doorway, but before I could follow she had pulled the door shut and led me toward the next room.

"Make yourself at home here, Ginny." Delores stepped to the sliding doors and opened a drapery to reveal a breathtaking ocean view.

As I stood inhaling the fresh salt breeze and listening to the roaring waves, I saw a surfer skimming shoreward. He hunched on a yellow pencil-slim shaft like a crouching lion, while behind him the keel of his board slashed white arcs in a surging avalanche of water.

"Who's that?" I pointed, although I expected the vision to disappear from sight at any moment.

"That's our neighbor, Liho Kalaka," Delores answered. "You'll probably meet him tonight."

"But he's marvelous, Dee! How he dips and glides!"

"Ginny." Something in Delores' tone distracted my attention from the dark-skinned performer. "Ginny. One thing. Make yourself at home here, but remember, I saw Liho Kalaka first."

Abruptly Delores left the room, and I heard her light step on the stairs. Looking back toward the sea, I could find no trace of Liho Kalaka. The vast emptiness where he had been was almost as frightening as Delores' words. *I saw him first.* The warning clanged like a bell in my ears. Delores had been sincere moments ago when she spoke of her feeling for Blaine. Surely she wasn't contemplating a new romance. My feelings were muddled, but suddenly I had no desire to meet Liho Kalaka that night or any night.

Davao had placed my bags on a long low luggage rack, but unpacking could wait.

Kauai beckoned. I opened the wrought-iron grill outside the sliding doors and stepped onto the balcony which overlooked the front entrance to Hale Malani and beyond that, the ocean. Like dark lashes, a circle of palm fronds outlined the greenish eye of the sea, and I stood hypnotized as the surf rushed upon the sand, relaxed, then foamed into a froth of white. I could hardly wait to put on my bathing suit, go to the deserted beach, and relax on the soft sand.

Sudden quarreling voices shattered the silence, and I tensed. It was unlike Delores to shout at anyone, yet I recognized seething anger in her words. Although Pindora Thal lapsed into a foreign tongue, there was no mistaking the fury in her tirade. Remembering Davao's hint about seeing my fill of Kauai in a short time, my first thought was that the Thals were angry at having a houseguest, at having another person to cook for and to clean up after. Perhaps my welcome at Hale Malani was cooler than Delores had led me to believe.

CHAPTER THREE

Wanting to give Delores time to recover from her squabble with Pindora, I stepped back into the redwood-paneled bedroom, kicked off my blue pumps, and began unpacking. The green tiled floor cooled my stockinged feet as I padded from my suitcase to the walk-in closet where I hung up my mainland clothes beside the one gay muumuu I'd had time to purchase at the Honululu airport.

After arranging my toilet articles on the koa-wood dressing table, I freshened up in the bathroom adjoining my room, slipped into the green and gold holomuu that Delores had sent me last Christmas, and wandered again onto the balcony where the hypnotic sound of the water soothed me. Tomorrow I would swim and swim and swim some more.

Sunshine toasted my face and arms as I relaxed in a bucket chair, and I could almost taste the tangy salt breeze that wafted all unpleasantness from my mind. This was what I needed, rest and release with nothing more serious to consider than the endless waves. I jumped when Delores tapped on my open door and quashed my dreams with reality.

"Whatever is keeping you, Ginny? I'm dying to hear about New York. If you're trying to sneak in a nap before dinner, forget it." Peering through the room to the balcony, Delores joined me. "You'll have the whole endless night for sleeping."

"I'm not napping, just devouring the view. What a paradise! How lucky you are, Dee."

"Once upon a time I knew." Delores sounded like a wistful child, and dropping into a chair beside me, she stared at the ocean. I knew she was thinking of Blaine, of a paradise lost; I had no right to call her lucky.

"Tell me about Hale Malani, Dee. It's so unusual. Surely there are some special stories or legends about it."

"None that I've heard. It's been in Blaine's family since the 1930's. Years ago their formal country home was in the Diamond Head area on Oahu, but Honolulu soon mushroomed around it. Blaine's father built this villa as a vacation retreat."

"Just a temporary beach shack." I laughed and touched the massive rough stone wall behind my chair.

"Native rock," Delores said. "These very islands are huge mounds of lava, and the redwood you see on the house does resist termites. For all its massiveness Hale Malani is really quite a practical structure for this tropical climate."

"Do the Malanis still vacation here?"

"No." Delores brushed an imaginary wisp of hair from her pale forehead. "The villa was our wedding gift, and Blaine was trying to work the land. Managing the hotel, the Royal Poinciana, ate up great chunks of his time, but even though he was a tyro at any sort of farming, his father's pineapple plantation always fascinated him."

"That's the family occupation, then, pineapple growing?"

Delores nodded. "But Father Malani wanted Blaine to expand the family holdings, to develop the hotel into Kauai's finest tourist resort. Blaine had other ideas. He enjoyed the intricacies of hotel management, but he was eager to develop an improved pineapple. He hoped to revolutionize the industry."

"But how?" I asked. Delores spoke in a faraway, dreamy voice, and I encouraged her, hoping that she might reveal some of the thoughts that troubled her, some of the fears that must be clinging in her mind.

"Blaine experimented with special plants, Ginny. I suppose it's presumptuous of me, but I'm trying to continue his work. He left instructions, but it's a struggle to get Davao to follow them."

"Have the Thals always lived at the villa?"

"Yes, ever since it was built." Delores rose and strolled around the corner of the balcony, and as I heard her gasp of surprise, I hoisted myself from the depths of the low-slung chair.

"What's the matter, Dee?" I spoke only seconds before I saw the huge, wood-carved figure blockading the narrow side balcony.

Delores managed a whispery laugh. "Drat that thing! I know it's here, but I seldom come this way, and it always surprises me."

I walked to the spot where the brown, larger than life-size image stared with unseeing saucer-eyes toward the ocean, its monstrous mouth half-mooned into an evil, mocking smile.

"Friend of the family?" As I touched the rough, carved surface with my forefinger, I smelled the musty odor of the weathered wood.

Delores shuddered. "No friend of mine. It's an ancient amakua god, and the local connoisseurs say it's authentic too. In pagan days these beauties guarded the sacred temples. Blaine kept this one up here as a tourist attraction."

"But I thought the villa was away from the sight-seeing area." I squeezed behind the forbidding figure to view it from another angle.

"Tourists seldom drive this way, but a daily excursion boat passes along the reef. It's equipped with a powerful glass, and the passengers enjoy peeking at Hewahewa."

"You've named him?"

"Blaine's idea. In ancient times a hewahewa was a respected high priest. This fellow will soon be gone, though. Mother Malani has invited him to Oahu to guard her garden gate. Davao's supposed to be making arrangements to have him shipped to Honolulu."

We wandered toward the back of the house, and I studied the distant mountains where green jewel-toned slopes gleamed in shafts of sunlight and lofty mountain peaks pierced gray rain veils.

As we returned to the side balcony, I noticed two cottages almost swallowed by a jungle of tropical vegetation. "Who lives in those houses down by the beach?"

"Come on. I'll brief you on our neighbors while we eat."

Stepping back into my bedroom, I was surprised to see a small figure dressed in gold sandals and a yellow holomuu bending over some garments on my bed. At first I thought it was Pindora, but as the girl looked up, I saw that she was quite young and beautiful.

"Nona, wonderful!" Delores pulled me toward the bed. "Ginny, I want you to meet my seamstress, Nona Ying. She's been working hard to have these muumuus ready for you."

"Nona. It's nice to meet you. I had no idea there was such a surprise in store." I fingered the smooth cotton in the three bright garments. "They're lovely! Such color!"

"Miss Ginny try them on?" As Nona Ying glowed under my praise, the slight flush on her cheeks heightened her beauty.

With Delores' help I slipped into the muumuus one by one and modeled each in front of the dressing-table mirror. They were lovely, they fitted perfectly, and the workmanship was exquisite. I elected to wear the yellow ankle-length sheath to dinner, and I slipped on my green silk turban to cover my hair.

"Nona, your work is outstanding. I've a roommate in New York who would absolutely drool if she could see me now. Could I engage you to make her a dress?"

"Nona's booked far in advance, Ginny. Perhaps sometime before you leave . . ."

"Will do. Will do." Nona interrupted Delores and smiled at me, and I knew I had made a friend. "Tomorrow I work for Miss Swanson, then I return to Hale Malani if it is your wish."

We made arrangements, and as Nona hurried away I tried to thank Delores for her thoughtfulness.

"Just an aloha gift, Ginny. Hope you enjoy them. But say! You really made a hit with Nona. She has a long waiting list. She's impulsive, but she'll keep her promise to you." Delores helped me hang the muumuus in my closet, then we headed downstairs. "I suppose you heard my quarrel with Pindora?"

"I'm sorry, Dee. If I've galvanized a servant rebellion, I'll move to the hotel."

"Heavens, no!" Delores sighed. "The problem's the opposite of what you're probably thinking." In the kitchen she opened the refrigerator, removed two artistically arranged fruit plates and scooped a mound of sherbet into the center of each.

"Before Blaine's — accident I prepared all the meals. Pindora managed the house. But now she's convinced that I need rest, and she's determined to take over the cooking. That's what we fussed about. Ginny, you can see it my way, can't you? I'll go batty here with nothing to do. Preparing three meals a day for five adults will take up at least part of my spare time."

Although I welcomed the minuscule flash of determination that sparked Delores' voice for an instant, I hesitated to side against

42

Pindora. "Five people to cook for?"

"Yes. Davao, Pindora, you, me, and Ward."

"Ward?" I tried to keep the curiosity from my voice. "Blaine's brother lives here *all* the time?"

"Only temporarily." Delores handed me a frosted pitcher of iced tea complete with golden spears of fresh pineapple, and with mouth watering I inhaled the sweet, fresh aroma as I followed her out to the lanai table that overlooked the ocean.

"During the school year Ward teaches part time in New York while earning his doctorate in composition. He needed a place to work for the summer, and since Father Malani has practically disinherited him, Mother Malani persuaded Blaine to extend him a sub-rosa invitation to live here with us. His room's at the head of the stairs, and there's a piano there; we'll hear plenty from him before he leaves, which with any luck at all will be in two weeks. But tell me about New York. What really happened?"

Forgetting Ward for the moment, I paused, my fork in midair. A few hours ago New York had seemed a maze of cul-de-sacs, but now, sitting here on an open terrace several thousand miles away, the city seemed less formidable.

"It's the same dreary story, Dee. Small-town girl dances to the big city, stubs her toes on the bright lights, and stumbles back home."

"Was it that bad, Ginny? Aren't you ever going back?"

"Trying to ditch me already?" I teased, then I smiled at the consternation on Delores' face. "Don't worry, Dee, you're stuck with me for a while, and how can I ever thank you for landing me a singing job at this hotel, the — what's its name?"

Delores squeezed lime juice into her tea. "The Royal Poinciana. But don't change the subject. What actually happened in New York?"

I removed a lavender orchid from my half shell of papaya and tasted the sweet fruit. "Things began well enough. I rated a chorus job in an off-Broadway musical, but the opening night audience deserted during the first act — walked out like shoppers who'd just got wind of a bargain-basement special across the street."

"That must have been tough," Delores agreed.

"Through that experience I did get an audition with the Melodeers. We did some local television before they disbanded, but nothing caught on. Then I took every cent I had saved, hired a combo, and made a pilot recording. It flopped. So here I am, the gal who thought singing a failure-proof occupation, finished."

I didn't tell Delores that Matt, Professor Jackson, had begun to ask me out socially and that I welcomed this chance to escape his attentions. I liked Matt, but I couldn't let him find out about the real me. I wanted to forget him along with my recurring dream that had assumed nightmare proportions in the past few months.

"So let's forget New York," Delores said. "Your job at the Royal Poinciana will be a snap. The tourists only want to hear the island melodies, and you can memorize a complete repertoire in no time. Ward'll help you as soon as he returns. He works at the hotel too, you know. In fact, you're his replacement; but you'll share the spotlight with him until he leaves."

I stabbed a slice of mango with my fork while Delores began eating her sherbet. "Where is Ward?"

"His dad's in Hilo on business, so he's visiting his mother for a few days. She's redoing their town house in the decor of the early mission homes, and she wanted his advice as well as his company."

"Were the Malani ancestors missionaries?"

"Ward's great-grandmother was the daughter of one of the first New England mission families to reach Hawaii. She broke all the rules of her day by marrying a Hawaiian, but the social mores are less strict today. All missionary descendants are top society in the islands."

"The idle rich?"

"Rich, but about as idle as a hill of ants." Delores refilled our tea glasses. "Most of the old families are active in sugar or pineapple, but many of the younger men serve the islands through politics. Blaine had planned to run for a seat on the legislature. Of course, Ward is different. Father Malani considers him a ne'er-do-well, but he's really a serious musician."

Although Delores spoke highly of Ward, I caught the coolness in her tone and I quashed my desire to ask more about him. After the way she had reacted to my mentioning the letter she had written, I knew I would have to work subtly if I were to be of any help to her.

"Dee, those two beach houses. You promised to tell me about them. I thought you had no neighbors here."

"Neighbors we have. Liho Kalaka lives in the house mauka toward the mountains. He's the surfer you admired."

46

"Surfing's his occupation?"

"In sort of a desultory way. He's a beach-boy at the Royal Poinciana — speaks a carefully studied brand of pidgin, gives the guests surfing lessons, and rents boards, outriggers, and catamarans."

"And you're fond of him?"

Delores parried my question like an expert fencer. "You'll have to meet him, Ginny. He's been most helpful since Blaine's accident."

"In what way, Dee?"

"You'll think it strange, but Liho relays my orders on to Davao. He volunteered for the job after Pindora let it leak out that her husband ignored all orders from women. Blaine left written instructions for the care of his experimental pineapple plants, and Liho sees that Davao follows them."

Although Delores' explanation of Liho's activities at Hale Malani was too glib to suit me, I decided to reserve judgment until I had met the man, until I had seen them together.

"And the other house?" I asked.

"Ah, now there's someone you might care to meet." Delores spooned up another bite of dessert. "By the way, this is paho sherbet. It's made from a native fruit."

"It's delicious." I paused to encourage her

to finish telling me about her other neighbor.

"The mystery woman's a newcomer, a recluse."

I sensed Delores intentionally arousing my curiosity, but I was willing to humor her. "But who is she?"

"Bette Swanson." Delores whispered as if revealing a secret.

"*The* Bette Swanson?"

"None other." Carrying our plates to the kitchen, Delores clattered them into the sink before she continued. "But don't get too excited. She says she's in retirement, but she's practically gone into seclusion, and she's prickly as a sea urchin. I'd perform introductions, but she snubs me. Your best bet for meeting her would be to 'accidentally' run into her on the beach. Or perhaps Nona could introduce you. She sews for her."

I could hardly imagine Delores failing to make friends with such a close neighbor. "I'd hate to intrude on her privacy," I said. "But Bette Swanson! How long did she sing at the Met? I'm sure she was famous long before I was born."

"I understand that she's divorced from a wealthy Boston industrialist and that she plans to live here permanently," Delores said. "Kapu signs have popped up like spores over her property, and she owns a feisty black Pekingese that yaps and snarls if anyone goes near her place."

"Kapu? That's a local term for keep out, right? She must be terribly lonely. I wonder what she does with her time?"

"Save your sympathy." Delores snickered. "Blaine hinted several times that Bette Swanson has a secret admirer — that she isn't as all alone as she pretends to be. Wait while I take these glasses to the kitchen, then we'll walk to the shore. I'll show you the best places to swim."

I fished a pineapple spear from my tea glass, then, sucking its fresh sweetness, I wandered into the yard and strolled among the flower beds. The heavy, sweet odor of gardenias mingled with the spicy fragrance of pink carnations to form an ambrosial perfume, but I strolled on toward a circular plot of white crown flowers that looked as if they had been carved from antique ivory.

As I walked I thought that the longer I was around my sister the more I noticed the change in her personality. Years ago if she even suspected that anyone disliked her, she made every effort to win them over. And she usually succeeded. Yet now she seemed strangely disinterested in one close neighbor, and all too wrapped up in another.

I walked farther than I had intended, and as

I paused to wait for Delores at the arched gateway to the Malani property I stood gazing at a narrow strip of red dirt that curved toward the ocean — now hidden behind dense tropical greenery. The kapu sign at the head of the path warned me that the lane must lead to Bette Swanson's home. Far to the left I saw another break in the tangled roadside thicket, and I guessed that this was another trail which probably angled toward Liho Kalaka's home.

I sank down on the grass in the shadows of the hibiscus and tall pines. I don't know how long I sat there resting and waiting before the bright flash of orange caught my eye. Someone was approaching on Bette Swanson's taboo trail. I scrambled to my feet, but the person slunk into the brush. My eyes probed the undergrowth. I saw no movement and heard no sound except the distant rush of the surf and the nearby rustle of palm fronds in the whispering breeze.

"Ready to go?"

I jumped as Delores' voice startled me.

"Surprise you? A phone call delayed me, but I guessed that you must have wandered toward the ocean. Believe me, it's easier going down than coming back. This looks like a gentle slope, but when we trek homeward, you'll think you're climbing Mauna Loa."

"Didn't you say that Bette Swanson forbids

people to use her private trail?" I asked.

"That's right. Why?"

"I just saw someone trespassing there — a man, I think. He disappeared into the thicket before I got a good look."

"Your imagination," Dee said. "If anyone were near, her pesky Peke would be yapping like crazy."

At that moment a tall figure emerged onto the main road from the farthest trail. If he hadn't been wearing a green aloha shirt, I would have guessed he was the same person I had seen moments before.

"Oh, Ginny! Sorry. We'll have to walk another time. Here comes Liho, and he probably wants tomorrow's instructions for Davao."

Handsome in a rough way, Liho Kalaka walked with an artless feline grace. Tucked behind his left ear, a sprig of green leaves drew attention to the smoldering black eyes, close set in his king-size head. Although sideburns and beard masked most of his face, I guessed him to be in his early twenties. The tropic sun had bleached tawny highlights into his shagged black hair, which curled in corkscrew tendrils on the nape of his neck. As he towered above us like a huge brown giant, I sensed a deep-seated arrogance in his manner.

Liho Kalaka was poised and seemingly pleased to see us, but after Delores introduced us, he reached up rather self-consciously and fastened the top button of his sport shirt. But I had already caught a glimpse of orange fabric showing at the neckline. A shiver tingled across the back of my neck; Liho Kalaka was camouflaging an orange garment. Perhaps Blaine Malani had been right. Maybe Bette Swanson did have a clandestine admirer.

CHAPTER FOUR

Liho Kalaka's presence could make almost any woman wonder if her nose were powdered and her lipstick fresh, and Delores was no exception. She patted at her hair and honored him with a glance that was almost worshipful.

I watched Delores come to life. Like a suddenly raised shade, the opaqueness vanished from her eyes, her smile brightened, and a rosy flush tinged her pale cheeks. I boiled with frustration at my own insufficiency; my arrival plus several hours of careful conversation had done absolutely nothing for my sister, yet the mere presence of this king-size Polynesian turned her on as easily and as quickly as if he had pushed a power switch.

What was going on here? Surely Delores hadn't fallen for this beachboy! I masked my feelings of inadequacy with my practiced smile as Liho pulled the sprig of leaves from behind his ear and presented it to me with a flourish.

"Mos' please t'meet haole wahine. More bettah I should come here sooner."

If the flow of uneducated pidgin that spouted from Liho's lips hadn't surprised me so, he might have hypnotized me with the aromatic forest perfume drifting from the greenery he had given me. His voice was deep throated and smooth as coconut syrup, and he made me feel as if I were the most attractive woman he had ever met.

"Save the local color for the tourists, Liho." Delores laughed. "Ginny's one of us now, and she's going to be working at the Royal Poinciana with Ward — and you." Delores hesitated over the last two words as if she hated to voice them, hated to admit they were true.

"Aloha, Ginny," Liho said simply. "Forgive the pidgin, but I'd hate to disappoint a tourist, they expect it you know."

"Liho, you've been picking maile again." Delores' tone was strangely accusing as she frowned at the leaves in my hand.

"These are special?" I sniffed the fragrant sprig and felt its crispness between my thumb and forefinger.

"Maile is hard to find these days," Delores said, "and the vines should be protected. The plant is so scarce that maile leis are used only on state occasions."

"These leaves were always a favorite of the royalty," Liho said. "I pick what is rightfully mine."

If Delores noticed the insolence in his words she chose to ignore it and to change the subject. "Liho, did you notice anyone on the path as you came here?"

"No. Should I have?" Liho's voice growled deep in his throat as he glanced over his shoulder.

"There was no one on Mr. Kalaka's path," I said. "But I saw someone on the other trail — the one leading to Miss Swanson's cottage."

"Perhaps you saw a Menehuene." When Liho grinned, his eyes almost disappeared in his handsome face.

"A what?" I asked.

"Pay no attention to him, Ginny. He's a joker and a tease." Delores spoke as if exasperated, but her adoring glance at Liho belied her words. "The Menehuenes are legendary elves who are supposed to have inhabited Kauai in pagan times."

"If this was a Menehuene, he'd taken vitamins," I said. "This person was tall."

"Impossible." Liho arrogantly dismissed my words as if I were an imaginative child. "If anyone was trespassing on Swanson property, that blackhearted Peke would have barked.

You probably saw a shadow, or perhaps a stray rainbow. The islands are full of gray mists torn by sudden shafts of brilliant light."

I let Delores and Liho believe that he had convinced me, but I knew I was not mistaken. Liho walked between us with self-assured grace as we climbed up the slope toward the formidable brown villa. When we reached the flagged terrace he dropped into a chair without invitation leaning his huge head back until the soft yellow cushion settled above his tawny-streaked hair like a golden crown. Liho seemed very much at home, and once again I felt uneasy — felt a presentiment of disaster.

"Delores, I came to get Davao's instructions. I'm booked to take a party of Royal Poinciana guests surfing before their nine o'clock canyon tour, and I guessed that you'd rather be undisturbed so early in the day. If I recall correctly, Davao should start treating the oldest plants with iron-zinc solution tomorrow."

"I'll check on it for you." Delores started to go inside, then hesitated as if reluctant to leave Liho and me alone.

"I'd love to see those pineapple plants when Davao isn't around," I said. "Is there time tonight?"

"Don't let that gruff old spook scare you."

Liho darted me a supercilious smile, and his teeth gleamed white against the bronze tan of his face. "He hides behind a bantam rooster bluff. Delores only humors him because he's been with the family for ages."

"Davao scares me too," Delores said with a laugh. "Come on, let's go see the beds now. He and Pindora should be settled in their rooms for the evening. I'll look up those instructions when we return."

Indisputedly in charge, Liho led the way around the villa, and while Delores clung to his arm as if she feared he might escape, I shrank from his touch when he tried to guide me by the elbow. We paused at a small grove where I examined unusual trees which sent out both gray tentlike bases of aerial roots and bright green leaves that resembled willow or bamboo. Then I saw the greenish oval-shaped fruit hanging like barrel lanterns among the leaves.

"Blaine raised pineapples on trees?" A sharp leaf edge raked my hand as I stretched to touch one of the spiny fruits.

"Is da tourist pineapple." Liho grinned, pleased with his patronizing pidgin. "Hawaiians no eat da kine Pandanus fruit."

Delores smiled as if Liho's words were gems, then we ducked under the tree branches and headed to the other side of the

57

Pandanus grove. A short distance away, in back of a brown utility shed which was choked by a strangling growth of wood-rose vines, I saw the pineapple rows.

"Disappointed?" Delores asked.

I rearranged my expression. "Well, I was expecting — more of them, I guess. There can't be over a hundred plants here."

"A fairly accurate estimate," Delores said. "But remember these are scientific beds, not industrial fields. Each row, and sometimes each plant, represents a stage of experimental development."

The dusky blue-green leaves of the low-growing plants surmounted the golden tones of the ripening fruit, and a saccharine fragrance that reminded me of cozy kitchens and upside-down cake sweetened the air.

"Had Blaine learned anything from all his testing?" I asked.

"Yes," Delores said. "He was close to having worthwhile information for the Research Institute. With Liho's help Davao should be able to complete the experiments."

"It all sounds terribly important." I hoped my perfunctory remark would hide my lack of a more intelligent comment.

"Pineapple's big business," Liho said. "Total pack amounts to about thirty million cases of juice and fruit. Other parts of the plant are processed into livestock feed and other by-products."

I merely nodded in response to Liho's burst of information. His voice had grown tense as that of a child reading unfamiliar words from an adult book, and his speech had lost all vestige of the fluid accents that marked it earlier. But he glanced at his watch and fell back into character just as I was beginning to wonder at a beach boy having such a wealth of information about the pineapple industry.

"Delores, perhaps you will get the instructions now." Liho's words suggested, but his tone commanded. He glanced at his watch a second time. "I'm due at the Royal Poinciana in a few minutes."

"Do you surf at night?" I asked as we returned to the villa.

Liho shook his great head. "This evening I'm taking two haole malihini couples on a moonlight sail."

"Sounds like a romantic treat for the white visitors." I suspected that Liho wanted me to be puzzled if not awed at his Hawaiian phrases, and it pleased me to let him know that I understood them.

"Romance for them, money for me." Liho shrugged his shoulders.

"Liho tries to sound crass and commercial," Delores said, "but he'd rather surf and sail than eat. Show Ginny your medal, Liho. A few years ago he was grand champion in the Hawaii Surfer's International sponsored by the Honolulu Surfing Club."

"It is nothing." Liho fingered the copper surfboard medal, then held up another yellowish-white trinket that he also wore on the copper chain around his neck.

"I am proud of the medal, but it's one any good surfer might win. This whale's tooth is another matter."

Delores looked embarrassed, but I willingly asked the question he expected from me. "What does the whale's tooth signify?"

"It's the mark of royalty." Arrogance rang in Liho's voice. "My ancestors wore this chunk of ivory on a cord of braided hair — hair from the heads of their friends. I am honored to wear a talisman which I consider kapu for haoles as well as for most Hawaiians."

Delores seemed relieved when we reached the villa, but even her pretext of shushing us so we wouldn't disturb Davao and Pindora failed to distract me from Liho's boasting, and again I felt a foreboding of danger. His braggadocio masked poorly concealed animosity, but toward whom it was directed, I was unsure.

As we walked in the back entrance and padded through the kitchen toward the drawing room, I heard the stealthy closing of a door. I peered over my shoulder to see who had been watching us, but although no one was in sight, I knew that either Davao or Pindora was nearby. Delores seemed not to notice. It had grown dark, and she flipped on a light in the shadowy front foyer, then paused before the gilt-framed portrait that I had noticed earlier.

"Who's the regal lady?" I asked.

"That's the islands' last monarch, Queen Lililuokalani." Delores smiled. "She guards our treasure."

Delores joked, yet I sensed Liho grow tense as a bow string. I thought Delores was joking until she shoved the gold-framed painting aside to reveal the black and silver combination lock of a wall safe.

"How dramatic." I listened to the steel knob whisper as Delores gave it a spin. "Your cache for the crown jewels, no doubt."

"It is a bit overdone," Delores said, "but Blaine always insisted that the data on his experiments be kept in the safe. I believe the precaution was more to guard against loss than against theft. It's a great idea as long as I remember the combination."

Delores gripped the metal knob again and spun the dial to the right, to the left, then back to the right again. Liho had been pacing like a caged lion back and forth across the foyer, but now as Delores dialed the combination, he paused in front of the mirror opposite the safe.

Instinctively I planted my body like a shield between the safe and the mirror. But when I turned, I found Liho merely combing his hair and preening at his reflection.

Delores handed Liho one sheet of paper from the sheaf in the safe and, laying it on a table, he read it, penciled a few notations in the awkward manner of a left-handed writer, and tucked it into his pocket.

As Liho left the villa, I was ready to apologize to Delores for being so suspicious of her friend, but when I looked at her, my words died. She had sagged into a chair as if exhausted, and she languished before my eyes. Her animation had disappeared with Liho Kalaka. Her eyes stared at me blankly, and I doubt that she would have heard me had I spoken.

I was so intent upon Delores that I had heard no one enter the house, yet I knew Ward Malani must have returned because the sound of piano playing poured into the night. Why hadn't he made himself known? I was about to ask Delores when Nona Ying called to me from the terrace.

"Miss Ardan, may I speak, please?"

"Certainly, Nona. Come join us."

Nona approached our chairs but remained standing.

"What is it, Nona?" Delores asked in a far-away voice.

"Miss Ardan, your turban interests me. It is most unusual."

"My New York roommate designed it, Nona. I'm pleased that you like it."

"Is a secret, the design?" Nona asked.

"Of course not. Would you like to study it?" I removed the turban, smoothed my hair, and handed the scrap of green silk to Nona who examined it inside and out.

"Miss Swanson, she asks me to make her a turban. I try, but none suit. Perhaps this pattern would please her. With your permission I show it to her immediately."

"It's too late for calling tonight, Nona," I said. "Take it with you and keep it for as long as is necessary. Here. It's adjustable. Let me put it on you." I stood, fitted the green silk over Nona's jet hair, and stood back to admire the effect. Completely unconscious of her beauty, Nona patted the turban more firmly in place.

"Must go now. I thank you. Day after tomorrow I return here."

CHAPTER FIVE

I led Delores upstairs as one might help an exhausted child, and although I went to my own room, I fought sleep. Sleep and nightmares had become synonymous in my mind. With the glass doors closed my quarters were stuffy and hot, yet when I opened them the night sounds of the island invaded my privacy.

Balcony timbers creaked and groaned, and as the wind sighed under the pagoda eaves, I heard the hiss of palm fronds and smelled the salt air. In the distance the sea slapped waves onto the shore, then sucked the water back in preparation for another onslaught. Kauai was not the silent haven I had expected; now, at midnight, it seemed like some malevolent aquatic creature — dozing, yet subconsciously waiting to surge into violent action.

I pitched and turned all night, yet I must have slept because early the next morning I awakened to the sound of dissonant, Orientallike music. A single phrase droned monotonously, then a figured bass thumped an erratic beat. Ordinarily the disturbance would have irritated me, but today I wanted to get up; I could hardly wait to swim and then relax on the sand.

As I stood gazing from my balcony, the sun melted the ocean into shimmering molten silver, and I lifted my hand to shield my eyes from the splendor. But stepping around the corner of the balcony was like blundering into another world. Dark shrouds of rain cloaked the mountain tops, and a gray mist turned the vegetation on the lower slopes into a dull, moss-colored slipcover. I hurried back into my room more determined than ever to soak up the beach's sunshine before it disappeared.

Wriggling into my new avocado-green bathing suit which the clerk had assured me "did things" for both my figure and my carroty hair, I flung a white terrycloth robe around my shoulders and tiptoed toward the stairs, being careful to make no sound that might alert Ward Malani. I was curious about him, but I had no desire to instigate an impromptu meeting at this early hour. The piano playing continued, and I gained the safety of the lanai before Pindora challenged my exit.

"Missy Ardan, you no leave before the

breakfast?" Like a pouting butterfly, Pindora frowned at me from the entryway.

"I'm only going for a short swim and a quick sunbath, Pindora. It's so early I hated to bother Delores or — or anybody."

"I hear you up. I fix cereal, juice, toast. Come."

Although I had never considered a hearty breakfast an infallible panacea, I relented. Pindora's tone brooked no argument, and as she fluttered toward me, her full bright skirt flying, I decided to avoid unpleasantness by humoring her.

Pindora carried my tray to the terrace and waited for me to sit down. Perching opposite me, she watched my every move until I self-consciously sloshed orange juice onto the front of my robe. Only a passing helicopter momentarily diverted her attention.

"Who's that?" I asked, more to make conversation than to gain knowledge.

"Tourists, Missy. They fly toward the Na Pali coast where roads have yet to go. The pilot, he let them off to picnic on a mos' private beach. Perhaps, Missy, you soon take the trip. Soon, before you leave here."

Again I was conscious of the reference to my leaving, but as I circumspectly studied Pindora's benign face I saw no artifice.

"Perhaps." I watched the helicopter until it

disappeared like a huge black bird behind the green cliffs that guarded the shoreline to my right. Then, finishing my juice and toast, I stood up.

"Thank you, Pindora. When Delores gets up, please tell her I'm on the beach."

"Yes, Missy. To your far right is public lane which leads to ocean. Use it and no one will mind."

Thanking Pindora again, I wondered why Delores had such problems with her. She seemed both helpful and pleasant. Then I laughed to myself, remembering how she'd badgered me into eating a breakfast I didn't want. Perhaps Pindora, like everyone else, was tractable enough as long as she had her own way.

I strolled to the main road, then turning, I followed the ribbon of asphalt to the dirt path that angled toward the sea. The powdery brick-red dust cooled my toes as it puffed around my thongs, but the sun warmed my head and shoulders. I followed the twisting trail through an ekoa thicket and on into a tunnel of palms that formed a green archway to the white sand. I stooped to filch a fallen coconut and to give it a shake; I had read somewhere that an amateur could choose a good specimen by listening for the juices splashing about inside the shell. But I heard nothing, so I let the shaggy brown husk plop back onto the sand.

The beach was all that I had imagined it to be. I spread my robe several yards above the spot where incoming waves laced the sand as they swirled, frothing and seething around the rocks.

Shedding my sandals, I splashed into the surf and felt the forceful, sensuous play of water against my skin. With the tip of my tongue I tasted the brine that sprayed my face, then I dived under an incoming breaker and swam out beyond the shallows.

I felt buoyant as I floated on my back, rolling gently with the swells. Since childhood I had loved to swim, and now I wished that Delores had more enthusiasm for the water. We needed a shared activity.

With sure strong strokes I swam parallel to the beach for a way, then I headed back for shallow water, letting myself drift with the tide. Feeling the shifting sand under my feet again, I steadied myself, then floundered through the churning surf back to the beach.

I flopped onto my robe and lay on my back until the sun flailed my skin, then turning, I covered my head with a tail of terrycloth and erased all disagreeable thoughts from my mind. But much as I wanted to continue this pastime, I was frustrated; Delores' letter haunted me. It was unlike her to fear people, and I couldn't believe that she had written the words as hastily as she claimed.

But the thing that bothered me most was her insinuations. Clearly, she was wary of the Thals, and she had implied that Blaine's death was an enigma. Then there was Liho. No matter what devotion Delores claimed for her late husband, I knew that this arrogant beach boy was more to her than a kindly neighbor.

Unable to enjoy myself with such a welter of thoughts in my head, I sat up, determined to plan some action. There was much I needed to know about my sister and her friends. Only when Delores' mind was at ease could I relax and perhaps fool myself into thinking that by helping her I had expiated my own cowardice in running to Kauai.

I shook the sand from my robe, and though I had every intention of returning to Hale Malani, I couldn't resist exploring a nearby rocky, almost inaccessible portion of the beach. Here the smooth white sand burgeoned into a rugged coastline, and I promised myself that I would only peek beyond the first rocks.

I stepped over jagged lava and picked my way toward the crags, enjoying the smell of the salt air and the feel of the silky sand slipping over my feet. Climbing a high crest of boulders, I perched on a rocky ledge overlooking a small cove and shallow pool. For one foolish moment I tried to blot out the horror — tried to tell myself that someone was swimming in the pool. Then I froze, still as the lava ledge supporting me. It was Nona Ying. Although she floated face down in the shallows of the low tide, there was no mistaking the yellow holomuu and the green turban that undulated at the side of the fanning black hair. It was Nona. And she was dead.

I was so numb with horror that I failed to see the huge breaker until it was almost upon me. I veered quickly, but my sandal caught in a crevice, and the force of the wave swept me down into the pool. I felt my ankle twist and a sharp pain stabbed my leg before the water receded. I lay beside Nona's body stunned and choking for several moments, but before another wave broke, I managed to drag myself from the pool and onto the sand.

I was helpless, but Nona Ying was beyond all aid. Terror threatened to overcome me, but pain forced me to take action. Although I was sure that my ankle was either broken or sprained, I thought I could grind my teeth against the pain and hobble home. I was wrong. Each jolt lanced my leg with shafts of flame. I could shout, yet I knew the surf would muffle my cries.

What had happened to Nona? Had she fallen? Was she pushed? Had she come to the beach at night, or had this happened to her earlier this morning? Was I in danger?

Liho Kalaka! If I could drag myself to his cottage, he would call Delores, call the police, call a doctor. I tried not to think of Nona. My stomach churned as I forced myself, sometimes hopping, sometimes crawling for what seemed like miles. The smallest outcroppings of rock were insurmountable mountains, and the soft sand was a trap designed to slow me. By the time I reached the beach fronting Bette Swanson's cottage, I was exhausted. Ignoring her predilection for privacy, I crawled into her front yard and yelled for help.

My voice had barely shrilled when the air exploded into a furor of yapping and barking, and a black bullet of determination hurtled toward me. I wrapped my sweaty arms around my sand-scraped knees and ducked my head to meet the attack. But my fear was needless. A brassy voice boomed, the Pekingese subsided, and I looked up at Bette Swanson.

For a moment she stood immobile, like a leviathan trapped in an invisible net. Although camouflaged in an ankle-length muumuu, her bulk astounded me, and as I

71

started, nonplussed, she spoke.

"Who are *you?* What are you doing here?"

"Nona Ying. Nona Ying's dead. I must call . . . someone." My voice sounded like a stranger's, and Bette Swanson stared at me, unbelieving.

"Who *are* you? What are you saying? *Nona Ying?*"

"I'm Ginny Ardan, Delores Malani's sister." I fought to control my voice. This woman had to believe me. "I found Nona Ying in a shallow pool among the crags. I must call the . . . police, but my ankle . . ."

The color drained from Bette Swanson's face, then with great effort she bent to help me to my good foot. "Brace yourself on my arm and we'll go to the lanai and see how badly you're hurt."

The few feet to Bette Swanson's terrace seemed like as many blocks, but we made it, and she eased me into a chair next to a low table tumbled over with scrapbooks.

"I'll call the police, then Dr. Niilonu." Bette Swanson eyed my melon-size ankle. "If what you say is true, we'll both be in for some questioning."

In the sitting position my pain abated somewhat, and I relaxed enough to notice the sweet scent of plumeria which saturated the terrace, and to wonder why Bette had said we'd both be questioned. I closed my eyes for a moment to try to think, but thought was impossible. A vision of Nona Ying haunted me.

When Bette Swanson returned from the telephone, I noticed details of her appearance for the first time. Her bulky figure and theatrical makeup were like a blight on the natural beauty of the flower-decked lanai. Her bleached, straw-textured hair and her sooty false eyelashes were as misplaced in this splendor of orchids and anthuriums as a Cracker Jack prize in a Tiffany setting. A cigarillo dangled like a brown straw from the red gash that was her mouth, and she squinted one watery eye as a wisp of smoke clouded her vision.

"The police are on their way, but Dr. Niilonu can't come, honey. After we've talked to the officers, I'll drive you to Hale Malani. Your sister has a morning appointment with the doctor, and his receptionist says he'll see you then. You're to keep all weight off the injured foot."

"You knew Nona Ying, Miss Swanson. Why do you think someone wanted to harm her?"

"Now, now." Bette Swanson tried to soothe me. "I know you must be terribly upset, finding — the body, and all. But if what you say is true, it's a police matter, not a thing for us to speculate about."

"But she was so kind and . . . beautiful. Why? Why would such a thing happen to *her*?"

"So you're Delores' sister." Ignoring my words, Bette Swanson paced restlessly around the terrace, all the while observing me through bleary eyes. "You're nothing alike, are you? And you're a singer?"

She stopped prattling and let me answer the second question. I tried to follow her lead and not speak of Nona Ying. "A would-be singer, I'm afraid. I just didn't make it in New York and spent my last dollar on plane fare to Kauai."

"The Met retired me at age fifty. Perhaps we should form a club. I also left New York dead broke. Oh, I made enough money through the years, but come easy, go easy." Bette shrugged her shoulders.

"You're joking!" The idea of Bette Swanson being a failure was beyond imagination. "How I loved hearing you as Aida! And no one has surpassed you as Brunhilde."

The mention of the roles that she had played so grandly seemed to evoke memories of happier days. Bette Swanson opened a scrapbook, flipped quickly to the reviews of *Aida* and *Die Gotterdammerung*, then continued her pacing while I read the columns of

74

praise. I couldn't blame her for being proud. If I'd rated a few good reviews, I might still be in New York. But I couldn't keep my mind on trivialities.

"Had you seen Nona last night?" I asked.

"You've studied?" Bette Swanson made it clear that she wouldn't discuss Nona.

"Of course I've studied." With my thoughts on the horrible crag-rimmed pool, I summarized the highlights of my brief career, and Bette Swanson listened with interest. Could Delores be wrong about her? She seemed anything but a recluse. In spite of her bizarre looks, which turned her into a cheap caricature of her former self, she appeared to be an outgoing person, hungry to talk, yet eager to listen.

When I spoke of my frustration, Bette Swanson tossed me the surprise of my life. "Let me give you lessons, Miss Ardan. I can teach you some secrets — secrets I've guarded stubbornly for a lifetime."

"But Miss Swanson, I'd be intruding. Delores warned me that you want privacy. You mustn't disrupt your life for me. We'd probably never have met if it hadn't been for — Nona."

"But we did meet, and I'll help you even if you are that one's sister." She paused, then spoke with complete candor as she twisted

75

her hands nervously. "No, I'll be truthful. My desire to help is secondary to my need for an audience — even an audience of one, if that one is a trained musician. You can't imagine how, how *direful* it is to have grasped fame and then to have lost it. Be my audience. Listen to me. I'll teach you every trick I've learned. That's a promise."

"Miss Swanson, you hardly know me. My ability may disappoint you." I wanted to jump at her offer, but I hesitated to commit myself to anyone who spoke so disparagingly of Delores. Bette Swanson seemed pathetically sincere, but I wanted time to think before I made a decision one way or another.

"Consider my offer," Bette Swanson said. "Oh, here come the police."

Two grim-faced Hawaiians rounded the corner of the cottage and stepped onto the lanai. Bette Swanson motioned them to chairs, and I was surprised to see stark fear etched into every feature of her face. Officer Logella, a tall barrel-chested man, introduced himself and his partner, Officer Kapuli, who readied a notebook and held a pen poised in long slim fingers.

"We'll have to ask you a few questions," Officer Logella said, a grim smile crossing his tan face.

"Must you?" Bette Swanson paced nervously and gestured toward my leg. "Miss Ardan is injured — in pain. Surely the questions can wait."

"No." I surprised myself with my objection. "We've made arrangements with the doctor. I'll be all right until then. I want to help. Nona Ying was my — my friend. If anyone was responsible for her death . . ."

"You've known Miss Ying a long time?" Officer Logella asked.

"Only since yesterday." I realized my claim of friendship must sound phony.

"Surely Miss Ardan should see a doctor immediately." Bette Swanson continued her pacing.

"The questions will be routine and brief." Officer Logella inhaled until his shirt stretched tightly across his chest. "We found Miss Ying's body in the place you described, Miss Ardan. Her death seems to have been accidental. There was nothing at the scene to indicate otherwise. As nearly as we can determine, she fell, hit her head on the rocks, and pitched into the pool where she drowned. The accident probably happened sometime between ten P.M. and dawn. Of course there'll be tests . . ."

I shuddered. How could they be so sure Nona had fallen? What had she been doing on the beach at night? My mind shouted silent questions while I answered the officer's routine queries. When had I seen Nona last? Was she alone? Did she seem frightened? How did I happen to discover the body?

Although the officer had termed Nona's death an accident, and although the questions did seem routine, I had the sensation of being gently lured into a trap — of being led to say things that I might later regret.

I had all but forgotten my throbbing ankle while I was being questioned, but now that Bette Swanson was having her turn, my pain became sharper. I wasn't even hearing her words. I caught a sentence fragment that alerted me.

". . . saw her around nine o'clock. She came on business. Unusual hour? Yes. But she was an impulsive girl, and she was excited at finding a special design she thought I'd like. She'd been to Hale Malani, had seen my light, and had taken the liberty of stopping by."

After the brief questioning the officers offered to drive me to Hale Malani, but Bette Swanson objected. "I'll take her. It's settled."

Having expressed their thanks to us, the officers departed, and Bette Swanson seemed to come to life again. I wondered why she had been so frightened. Indeed, the questions had been routine. Too routine. A drowning following a blow on the head. Nona Ying had died in the same manner as Blaine Malani, but the officers had seemed oblivious to any coincidence. I needed to talk to someone, but whom could I trust?

Together Bette Swanson and I managed to get me onto my good foot. As I hobbled, leaning against her arm, I lurched against the table and sent the tumble of scrapbooks banging to the ground with pages and clippings flying like leaves in the breeze. Bette Swanson's face turned beet red as she jacknifed her bulk to retrieve them, and I apologized.

"Please, Miss Swanson, let me take your scrapbooks to Hale Malani and repair them. That would only be fair, and besides, I'd enjoy the opportunity of reading your press notices."

"You needn't make repairs, but I'll gladly loan the books. No one's been interested for ever so long; I'd almost forgotten the feeling. Let me take them for you."

Bette Swanson restacked the fallen books into a neat pile, then turned to help me just as a sharp pain pierced my leg. Averting my face to hide my tears, I saw an ashtray that had been lying under the books. It overflowed with cigarette and cigarillo stubs, and I noticed that only some of them bore red lipstick tattoos. Nona Ying had worn lipstick. I had noticed how it blended with her dress. Again I thought that Blaine Malani might have been right — that Bette Swanson must have a male companion. Last night I had been willing to believe that Liho Kalaka was Bette's secret visitor, but after meeting them both, I couldn't imagine that the handsome Liho would spend his time here.

CHAPTER SIX

Driving slowly in order to spare me unnecessary pain, Bette Swanson eased her luxurious red Cadillac along the kapu lane and on toward Hale Malani. Neither of us spoke, and I was glad the trail led nowhere near the spot where I'd discovered Nona Ying's body. Would I ever be able to swim on that beach again?

As we neared the villa, I saw Delores wander onto the terrace wearing a mauve-colored shift that emphasized her sallow complexion. From the expression on her face I knew she'd heard about Nona. She rushed to the car.

"Have you heard? Nona?"

I nodded, then a frown etched a V-groove of worry on Delores' forehead as she saw me try to hobble from the car.

"What's happened, Ginny?" Delores rushed to my side, nodded curtly to Bette Swanson, then helped me to a patio chair and knelt to examine my injured ankle. "Are you in pain?"

"It must be a twist — a sprain." I tried for a grin, but I knew it came out a grimace. "I fell when I saw . . . Nona. I found her there in that pool." I had to quit talking of Nona before I upset Delores, before I came unglued myself. "Miss Swanson rescued me, or I'd still be stranded down on the beach. She's arranged for me to accompany you to your doctor's office."

"Ginny! How terrible for you."

After squeezing her huge bulk from under the steering wheel, Bette Swanson carried her scrapbooks to the low coffee table beside my chair and gently arranged them, much as a mother might settle her baby in its crib. Except for one baleful glance, she ignored Delores, and I felt a current of animosity reverberating in the air.

"Entertainment while I mend," I said in answer to Delores' questioning gaze. "Miss Swanson's lent me the story of her life."

At that moment Davao backed the Malani limousine from the carport and, on seeing his cheerless face, Bette Swanson lumbered to her Cadillac, waved me a casual farewell, and then zoomed from the driveway before I could thank her properly for her help.

"You must really have impressed the great diva." Delores gave a disdainful snort as the red car disappeared.

"A stranger groveling on one's doorstep in

the early dawn — a stranger who's just dis-covered a dead body — is bound to draw a certain amount of attention, but other than that I did nothing except praise her singing. She was the greatest, Dee!"

"Perhaps she *was*." Delores emphasized the past tense. "But that must have been ages ago. She's a bit crude for my taste." Delores glanced from my ankle to her watch, then to the car. "Davao's waiting. Let's get you into something decent and be on our way. Oh, Ginny, I hope you haven't broken a bone! Just look at that swelling!"

"I'll have to go as I am, Dee. I could never make it up all those steps to my room." I ran my fingers through my disheveled hair, think-ing briefly of a green turban floating in seawa-ter.

Grim faced and noncommital, Davao watched while Delores sauntered back into the villa and returned with a muumuu.

"Here, Ginny. Shed that robe. Slip this over your swimsuit."

"Is that for street wear?" I eyed the tent-shaped garment with its beautiful, wild pat-tern of golden hibiscus blossoms splashed against a crimson and emerald background.

"It's the uniform of the islands — much more inconspicuous than your tailored city clothes."

The soft folds of the muumuu enveloped me, and I admired the Hawaiian penchant for comfort as well as beauty. Although Delores struggled under my weight as I hobbled toward the car, Davao offered no help. He sat as if transfixed behind the wheel and seemed put out to be chauffeuring two women, but when we were finally settled in the rear seat, he drove carefully toward the village.

We rode for several minutes before we spoke and, as if by mutual agreement, we avoided speaking of Nona. What was there to say?

"Dee, I didn't know you were seeing a doctor. Is it anything serious?"

"I think not." Delores relaxed against the car cushions as if she couldn't care less. "Dr. Niilonu prescribed some tranquilizers that gave me a rash, but since he changed my prescription, everything's been okay. You need him worse than I."

I murmured something casual, but my mind snapped to attention and I momentarily forgot my pain. Tranquilizers! That explained Delores' slow-motion, far-away-in-a-dream attitude. As I remembered her terse letter, I thought it quite possible that she needed me more than she realized: Perhaps her fears were merely being medicated into a limbo of lost nightmares. Was Nona Ying part of the nightmare? I was afraid to ask.

I watched Delores from the corner of my eye as we drove past clusters of cottages and endless acres of green cane fields. Then, as we turned inland, gained altitude, and drove alongside the darker, spruce-blue pineapple fields, I spoke again.

"It's almost beyond description, isn't it?" I motioned at the opulent scene, and nudged Delores into her role of hostess.

"I suppose the scenery does seem exotic to you," Delores said. "I guess I've come to take it for granted. But this is prosaic, just cane and pineapple. When your ankle mends, I'll show you Wiamea Canyon and Hanalei Bay. And you might enjoy a boat trip up Wialua River to the Fern Grotto. Everyone should see that."

My ankle throbbed again, and a wave of nausea threatened me. Sensing that I wasn't listening, Delores quit talking, and I breathed deeply until the squeamish sensation passed.

Davao drove directly to Dr. Niilonu's office, a low, ranch-type building outstanding for its brown lava-rock facade and shake-shingle roof. A monkeypod tree formed a living umbrella overspreading the front lawn, and masses of purple-blossomed vines bejeweled trellises on either end of the patio.

"Even the professional properties are exquisite," I said as Davao parked beside a border of flaming red shrubbery that rimmed the lawn like a scarlet ribbon.

"That's a rare beefsteak hedge you're admiring," Delores said.

"Rare? I saw several like it as we entered the village."

Delores smiled. "Rare as compared with medium or well-done. You'll notice some hedges are a pinkish shade and others are almost brown. But do come on. No sense in delaying the inevitable." Then, reconsidering, "No, you wait here. I'll be right back."

Volunteering no help, Davao remained behind the steering wheel, and I was relieved when Delores returned with a nurse and a wheelchair.

"This is Miss Yagakimo, Ginny. She'll trundle you inside."

I returned Miss Yagakimo's smile, and the two of them hoisted me from the car to the chair, then rolled me into Dr. Niilonu's waiting room. A potpourri of medicinal odors signaled the return of nausea, but I clenched my teeth and determined not to get sick.

If one could ignore the smell, the waiting room was pleasant enough. The bright cushions on the sisal furniture contrasted with the pineapple-colored walls and floor, and vases of waxy red anthuriums enhanced the gay decor.

Miss Yagakimo wheeled me into an examination room, and in a matter of minutes the tall, craggy-faced Polynesian doctor joined us and expressed his sorrow at Nona Ying's accident. His manner was both sympathetic and professional, and although his touch was gentle, I winced as his fingers examined my ankle.

"Is it broken?" Delores' voice shook.

"No, no. There's no fracture." Dr. Niilonu's voice had the sonorous quality of an Oriental gong. "But you do have a severe sprain. I'll bandage it, then we'll get you some crutches. You'll have to keep your weight off that foot for a week or so."

Relieved at Dr. Niilonu's prognosis, I clenched my teeth against the pain and watched as he worked with adroit efficiency until my ankle was neatly gift-wrapped. As I thanked him, Miss Yagakimo appeared with crutches, gave me instructions in using them, and helped me back to the outer office to wait for Delores.

I was exhausted when we arrived back at Hale Malani, and Delores willingly let Pindora serve us our lunch. Neither of us was hungry, but we pretended to eat until the sound of piano playing ceased and brisk steps clattered on the stairs.

Ward Malani strode onto the lanai like a

general preparing to review his troops, and Delores and I involuntarily saluted with a moment's silence. Ward stood straight as a lance, and his unusual manner of narrowing his eyelids gave his agate-colored eyes a hypnotic quality. When Delores finally remembered to introduce us, it was all I could do to respond. Ward's dark features were as rugged and homely as the khaki work clothes he wore, and his aura of businesslike efficiency was challenged only by the orchid blossom he had tucked into the buttonhole of his shirt. Delores made no mention of Ward's avoiding us the evening before.

"Afraid Ginny can't open at the hotel yet, Ward," Dee said as Ward joined us for lunch. "She's had a terrible shock, and she's sprained her ankle."

"I'm sorry to be such a bother," I said.

"Don't apologize." Ward offered no sympathy as he gazed at my ankle. "You can still open as scheduled."

"But how?" Ward's lack of understanding dumbfounded me. "On these crutches?"

"No problem," Ward said. "You'll sing sitting down. There's a mermaid costume somewhere around. You can wear that. We'll need all the time available if I'm to teach you any routines before I leave."

"You're responsible for my performance?"

I leaned forward in my chair.

"The new hotel manager let me end my contract early on the promise that I'd find my own replacement. You're it."

Ward's tone precluded argument, and I dreaded the thought of working with him. I had imagined that Hawaiians were all like Blaine had been — relaxed and friendly. And I had hoped that Ward might be able to answer some of my questions concerning Delores, Blaine, and Nona Ying. But after meeting him, I doubted that he was going to be of any help, and I could understand part of Delores' fear. I sensed that Ward Malani could be a powerful enemy.

I wondered in what way Delores had alienated Ward, but at least her eagerness to have him vacate Hale Malani was understandable. I too would be glad to see him go. Ignoring us both, Ward bolted his lunch and returned to his room.

In spite of the piano thumping, I escaped reality by napping the afternoon away in a reclining chair in the shade of the balcony on the side terrace. That evening after Delores and I finished dinner, I hobbled inside and fanned Bette Swanson's scrapbooks out on one end of the huge family room table, hoping they'd divert my mind from Nona Ying. And Blaine Malani. And murder.

"Ginny, you've lost a crutch tip." Delores twirled a red rubber cap on her forefinger, then fitted it onto the end of my crutch. "I'd better fix it before you slip and take a nasty fall."

"Does Pindora have some glue?" I asked.

Delores shrugged her shoulders and wandered toward the kitchen where Pindora clattered dishes into the sink. Presently she returned with a small plastic bottle of white glue.

"Here, I'll fix it." I squeezed a blob of adhesive into the rubber cap, eased it on the crutch tip, then laid it aside to dry. "Mind if I use the glue to repair these scrapbooks?"

"Be my guest." Delores yawned as she thumbed through one of the albums. "I have better books upstairs, Ginny. Like one?"

"No thanks, Dee. I find these fascinating."

"All right, but if you'll excuse me, I'll go on to my room."

I was deeply engrossed in Bette Swanson's press notices when I sensed an unwonted silence. Then I smiled; Ward had stopped playing. Moments later he stepped into the family room wearing white slacks and sport shirt, a blue and green tapa-print cummerbund, and a fragrant lei of yellow plumeria. I hardly recognized him.

"Off to work," he said.

"But you've been working all day," I replied. "I've heard you."

"I'm on at the Royal Poinciana tonight — that's the real job. This other is painful pleasure."

"The piano playing?" I asked. "Are you preparing a concert?"

Ward shook his head. "The Hawaiian Mission Children's Society has commissioned me to compose a suite for the Honolulu symphony." His eyes narrowed. "It's a great honor, but I worry that I'll be unable to produce anything worthwhile."

Ward now seemed relaxed and easy to talk to, and I wondered if Delores' presence at lunch had caused him to be so unapproachable.

"Delores says you're studying for a doctorate in composition on the mainland. Will this suite count toward your degree?"

"It may." Ward adjusted the yellow blossoms around his neck. "But that's really unimportant. The society wants a composition written by a 'native son' to be performed in Waikiki Shell in conjunction with Annexation Day festivities. This'll be my opportunity to prove to Father that I haven't completely deserted Hawaii by leaving Yale and working my way through music school."

Ward's words unconsciously revealed such

a poignant nostalgia and childlike earnestness that I forgot his earlier unchivalrous attitude toward my injury. In that fleeting moment I was almost drawn to him. Perhaps his earlier grim resoluteness had been only a mask — a protective armor that he wore when the need arose.

Ward suddenly looked uneasy, looked as if he realized he had said more than he had meant to, and he hurried from the villa. But I soon forgot Ward Malani as I followed Bette Swanson's career. At first, the reading had been pure pleasure; it was the Cinderella story of a beginner climbing the ladder of fame and fortune to a tower of glowing success.

Then the picture began to blur. Each year the clippings diminished in number and size and, toward the end, the reviewers were often either patronizing or unkind. In the most recent book Bette had inserted items irrelevant to her career, and it was pathetic to see the albums trace the path from her heyday to her stark demise.

Scattered like buoys in a shrinking sea of dubious reviews were motley items pertaining to friends — the wedding of a Sue Baldwin and a Lawrence Scott, the funeral of Mrs. Orrin Schoope, several birth announcements, then a notice of marriage license application for an Elizabeth Timmons and a Likeke Konapuno.

The hushed villa was suddenly depressing, and the tragedy told in the newspaper clippings saddened me. There was no denying the immutable fact that this is a winner's world, that society abandons losers to deal as they may with their loss and their loneliness.

I tried to shake the gloom that enveloped me, but it persisted even after I jolted up the stairs on my crutches and lay in bed listening to the steady beat of surf and wind. I tried to make plans for the next day, and although an exact course of action eluded me, I knew that before I could help Delores I had to learn the reason for her fear of Ward and her dislike of Bette Swanson. And I had to learn these things without arousing her suspicions.

CHAPTER SEVEN

The clatter of dishes and the pungent aroma of coffee awakened me the next morning. The familiar nightmare had disturbed my sleep and my eyes burned. Pulling a muumuu over my pajamas, I felt like the crooked man who walked a crooked mile as I hobbled downstairs and joined Delores and Ward at the family room table. With black eyes snapping, Pindora sailed about the kitchen in high dudgeon, and I suspected that she and Delores had been fussing again.

"That coffee smells delicious," I said. I had hoped for a leisurely patio breakfast, but intuition warned me that eating indoors had to do with Pindora's usurpation of Delores' cooking privileges. I hid my asperity behind a smile. Had I been the mistress of Hale Malani, I would have gladly delegated all culinary chores to the first willing person who crossed my path.

Ward rose, unconsciously smoothed his rumpled khakis, then pulled out my chair and leaned my crutches against the end of the long table where Bette Swanson's scrapbooks still lay scattered.

"Aloha!" Ward said. "How's the ankle?"

"Feeling much better, thank you." I reached for the cup of coffee that Delores poured from a silver pot.

"This coffee has a flavor all its own." I smiled at Delores, wondering how she could look so devastating this early in the morning and with no makeup to offset the somberness of her lava-colored robe.

"Kona coffee, Sis. Specialty of Hawaii — the big island." As Delores passed me a compote of iced pineapple wedges, a tray of buttered toast, and a pitcher of coconut syrup, the three fragrances mingled into a gourmet's delight.

"Missed your piano playing this morning, Ward," I said. "Frankly, I thought it would drive me crazy yesterday, but today the villa seems empty without it."

"Try to bear up." Ward shoved his chair back from the table and toyed with the golden plumeria blossom tucked in his buttonhole as he lingered over his coffee. "I'm taking the day off."

"A holiday? What's the occasion?"

"I intend to spend the afternoon teaching you the songs we'll use at the hotel tonight, but I'm afraid this morning is an 'I'm stuck' holiday." Ward scowled as if to deflect any commiserating.

"What's your problem? Perhaps I could help. I'd like to hear what you've written."

"Sorry." Ward dismissed my offer with a perfunctory shake of his head and gazed across the room through narrowed lids. "That's something I'll have to work out for myself."

Ward raked his chair back from the table, excused himself, and stamped up the stairway. Liho Kalaka arrived and I was diverted from Ward.

"How did you get along with Davao this morning, Liho?" Delores asked. "Any trouble?" She walked behind Liho's chair and rested her hands on his shoulders in a possessive gesture that disturbed me.

Liho patted her hand. "No trouble at all, Delores." Again he was the helpful neighbor. "Within a few days we'll start the final phase of treatments for the plants in the initial experimental group. Everything's on schedule."

Delores started to speak, but sounds of demolition from the kitchen caught her attention. She hurried toward Pindora's empire leaving Liho and me alone.

"What're all the clippings, Ginny?" Liho pulled one of the scrapbooks toward him.

"I've been reading Miss Swanson's reviews," I said. "In her day she was the greatest — a sun in a galaxy of stars. I admire her."

"To you she is *that?*" Liho idly flipped the pages in the book. "To me she's just a rich old biddy who spoils the beauty of Kauai with her powder and paint. I could show you more interesting things to do than to read yellowed clippings from the past."

Liho's voice was intimate, suggestive, and I was tempted to rise to his bait if for no other reason than to divert his attention from Delores. True, she had seen him first, but could she handle him? I hated the way she threw herself at him when he obviously had eyes for any female in his range. Also, I resented his callous appraisal of Bette Swanson, but I held my temper and tried to parry his veiled suggestion with dry humor.

"Well, since this ankle keeps me from my surfboard, I have to find other amusements. I sat up last night reading the scrapbooks until I'd finished every word. I found them most entertaining."

Liho was immediately all sympathy; I understood why Delores had fallen for his charm. He managed to convey the impression that I was a very glamorous female on or off crutches; and when I mentioned performing that night at the Royal Poinciana, he corroborated my unexpressed opinion that Ward Malani was a slave driver. It was all I could do to keep from agreeing with him, but I acted as if I were eager to begin work. Any other attitude would have made me seem disloyal to the Malanis, and although I resented Ward's no-nonsense attitude toward me, I felt it imperative that the family present a united front. Liho was an outsider. I chose to ignore his charm.

Stoically I rose, struggled onto my crutches, and demonstrated to Liho that I was perfectly capable of propelling myself about. I headed toward the lanai, then changed my mind, deciding to see how Pindora and Delores were getting along in the kitchen. As I turned unexpectedly, I saw Liho rip a clipping from the scrapbook he had opened, crumple it, and cram it into his pocket.

Quickly I veered back toward the terrace. Liho was unaware that I had witnessed his strange act, and for some reason I felt it would be dangerous to let him know. In a moment he followed me onto the terrace, complimented me on my agility, then said aloha and walked down the path toward his low-slung sports car.

I sunned on the side lanai until Delores brought my lunch. She was so oversolicitous about my ankle that it was all I could do to keep from answering her sharply. I was glad when Ward came downstairs carrying a record player and a stack of discs.

"If you two'll excuse me, I'll go upstairs for a nap." Delores yawned. "Don't worry about the noise — I think I could sleep through an earthquake."

Ward had brought combo recordings and printed word sheets to expedite learning the lovely Hawaiian songs. After I listened to a tune, he would sing it through with me. I found the repertoire easy to learn.

This job promised to be exactly what my craven heart was seeking — a no-challenge snap. Although the Hawaiian ballads were beautiful, there were no tricky rhythms or dissonant harmonies. As Ward said, all I had to do was to smile and sing.

We worked for over an hour then took a break while I copied lyrics on small file cards. Over frosted glasses of gin and guava juice I studied this aloof man who simultaneously attracted and repelled me. I had intended to confide nothing to Ward, but so much puzzled me that I decided to risk a few questions.

I wanted Ward's opinion of Liho, but I was afraid to ask. In supervising Davao, Liho performed a chore that Ward was evidently unwilling or unable to manage, and I thought that Ward might be jealous. Liho possessed a persuasive charm, and it was obvious that Delores was susceptible. Perhaps the animosity between Ward and Liho stemmed from pure jealousy.

"Ward, have you any doubt about how Blaine died?"

Ward's eyes narrowed. "Why do you ask that?"

"I might as well level with you. Right now Dr. Niilonu's tranquilizers keep Delores in a state of lethargy, but before I left New York she wrote me that she was afraid of something. Now that I'm here she refuses to discuss this, but she did hint that she doubted that Blaine's death was accidental. Now I wonder about Nona Ying."

"Nona? What do you think, Ginny?"

"How can what I think matter? I'm a newcomer. Delores and I have been separated a long time, but Ward, she's always been a person who attracted others. Has she changed? I only know what I feel, and I sense an undercurrent — a miasma of hostility. You and Delores are far from friendly, Bette Swanson ignores her, and Davao and Pindora eye her like menacing vultures. Nona Ying and Blaine were the only people I've met who liked Delores, and now they're both dead. Doesn't that seem strange to you?"

"You're letting your imagination fly, Ginny. Blaine had an accident. Nona had an accident. If there were any connection between the two, the police would have notified us."

"Then there's Liho Kalaka." I watched for Ward's reaction.

"What about Liho?" Cold as wet agates, Ward's eyes bored into mine through half-lowered lids, and I realized that he was treating my questions like hot potatoes, throwing them right back at me.

"That's what I wonder, Ward. What about Liho? It seems strange for him to give Davao orders. Shouldn't that be your job?"

Ward inhaled deeply as if he were going to tell me something, then we both heard the sound of bare feet slapping on the flagstones of the front lanai. A grubby dark-skinned boy with a flashing grin and an Oriental tilt to his laughing eyes hurried toward us, toting a plump plastic bag filled with yellow blossoms.

"Aloha," Ward called. "Are you hunting for Mrs. Malani?"

"No, sir." The boy thrust his burden toward Ward. "I am hired to give lei to the haole wahini, Ginny Ardan."

Ward handed me the bag, and before I recovered from my surprise, the boy ran from the lanai and disappeared behind the hibiscus hedge. I fumbled at the knot in the plastic, caressed the cool, golden blooms with my warm fingers as the heavenly fragrance wafted around us, then slipped the lei over my head. A white card fluttered to my lap, a card bearing four words in bold script: *Aloha also means farewell!*

"Yellow ginger!" Ward exclaimed. "You must have a secret admirer."

"There's no name." I held my thumb over the last three words as I showed Ward the card, and although I managed to keep my hand steady, I felt my heart pounding louder than the surf. There was no doubt. Somebody was politely but firmly telling me — warning me — to leave Kauai.

CHAPTER EIGHT

The trade wind ceased, and although the humid air was stifling, the coolness of the ginger blossoms against my skin sent chills to my fingertips. I slipped the card into the pocket of my muumuu, excused myself, and struggled upstairs. Once in my room with the door closed, I flung the lei at my bed, then stumped onto the balcony and flopped into a chair. The sun burned my skin, yet it failed to warm me. Someone wanted me to leave Kauai. Who? Why?

I went over a mental list of people whom I had met in my brief stay at Hale Malani. While Delores had invited me, and Pindora seemed to glow under the stimulation of another houseguest, I knew Davao would no more than lift an eyebrow if I packed and left within the hour. Who could guess at his plans?

Perhaps Bette Swanson resented my intrusion into her privacy and regretted her offer of voice lessons. Or maybe Liho wished to scissor me from the scene. If he were truly interested in Delores, he might well consider me an unwelcome chaperone.

Ward Malani? It was entirely possible that Ward wished to wage some personal vendetta against Delores without my interfering. I regretted revealing Delores' fears, regretted saying anything to this quiet, unfathomable brother of Blaine's. For all I knew it was Ward whom Delores feared most. Her comments about him on the day I arrived indicated that she tolerated him only for Blaine's sake — only because he was a Malani. My own questions to Ward had netted no answers; all I had done was to put him on guard.

I don't know how long I sat there before a terrorizing thought rose in my mind. Someone wanted to be rid of me. Someone wanted to be rid of me badly enough to kill me. Someone had tried and failed. Nona Ying lay dead because someone had mistaken her for me. I fought hysteria. The night Nona died both of us had worn yellow holomuus; and I had signed her death warrant by lending her my green turban, by fitting it onto her head and sending her into the night.

But why would anyone want to kill me? And who? I had no one to turn to. If only I could persuade Delores to leave Hale Malani, to come with me to the mainland! I wanted to hide in the seclusion of my room, and only the thought that I would be safe in a group persuaded me to go down to dinner. I didn't wear the appalling lei, and when Ward casually mentioned it, I even managed to smile at Delores' rather passive guesses as to the identity of my admirer.

"Perhaps Liho sent it to mark your opening at the Royal Poinciana," Delores said. "That would be like him; he's steeped in island traditions."

"If the lei came from that one I would shun it like a viper." Pindora's black eyes glittered like polished jet as she served her advice while passing an assortment of salad dressings. "He is the ladies' man, Missy Ginny. Save your heart for someone less fickle."

I saw Delores flush at Pindora's impertinence, and I tried to joke to avert a fuss. "Thanks for the warning, Pindora. Perhaps I'll carry a blue talisman to nullify Liho's charms. And Pindora, is there any more of that delicious pilaf? I'd love a second helping."

Pindora smiled and flew toward the kitchen, and Delores relaxed and seemed to forget the affront.

"Delores, I hope you're coming to hear us tonight at the hotel."

"You know I'd love to, Ginny, but I've

been nowhere since — for ages. I can't bear to meet people just yet. Give me awhile longer. You're going to be here indefinitely. I intend to see to that."

I couldn't help glancing at Ward as Delores spoke, but his face was an expressionless mask.

Glancing at his watch, he said, "Hate to rush you, Ginny, but we'd better be leaving. We're on at eight, and we'll have to allow time to get you zipped into that costume. It'll probably be the first time the public's seen an orange-tressed mermaid."

I ignored Ward, accepted more golden brown pilaf from Pindora, and thanked her with a smile. I hated Delores to stay home; a night out would have done her good, and I wanted her with me. I needed her. Somewhere on this island I had a deadly enemy. Perhaps it was Ward Malani.

Pindora beamed as I enjoyed her pilaf. Then, when I asked, she helped me upstairs. I wanted to allow Delores a few minutes in her own kitchen, but mostly, I wished to question Pindora.

Dusky evening permeated my room, and the cloying ginger scent drew my gaze toward the bed where shadows from the jungle growth of philodendron on the balcony rail transformed the redoubtable lei into an ugly mustard-colored stain on the counterpane. I snapped on the light.

"May I help you dress, Missy?"

"I'd appreciate that, Pindora. While I shower, will you lay out my white shift and red shoes, or shoe, I should say?"

On my good foot I hopped into the shower, washed quickly, then allowed Pindora to help me into the fresh clothing. When I was dressed I limped to the bed, picked up the lei, and held it toward her. "You take it, please. Wear it and look beautiful for Davao."

"Is from Liho, you believe?" Pindora inched backward, suddenly seeming much more like a caterpillar than a butterfly.

"I've no idea, Pindora. But now it is from me to you."

"The yellow ginger dies quickly." Pindora spoke in a trancelike whisper. "Is a symbol of — of briefness. I no like."

I had hoped to question Pindora about her comments on Liho, but she slipped away, leaving me holding the lei. I started to drop the blossoms in the wastebasket, but not wanting to return later to their cloying smell, I carried them to the balcony. I could hardly pitch them over onto the lanai so, bracing myself against the redwood railing, I limped to the carved amakua god and draped them about his umber neck.

On the drive to the hotel, Ward handled the Malani limousine with practiced ease and kept up a conversation as well. Was this man a murderer? I was glad we were expected at the hotel. I was safe as long as everyone knew of my whereabouts.

"The Royal Poinciana's still under construction, so it'll behoove us to provide good entertainment to compensate the guests for their inconvenience." Ward sat behind the wheel with military erectness and kept his eyes on the road.

"So that's how I got this job," I said. "I suppose regular entertainers refused to appear at a second-rate place."

"The Royal Poinciana's strictly first-rate," Ward said. "Just incomplete. It'll be the brilliant link in a chain of island hotels when it's finished. You got the job for the same reason that I did — because you're a Malani."

"But I'm not."

"You're Delores' sister. That's close enough." Ward slowed for a curve in the serpentine road, and I gazed through the twilight at an unobstructed view of ocean where a fringe of green palms and white sand beach ringed a small horseshoe-shaped cove.

Ward glanced at the scene and continued speaking. "The Royal Poinciana was another of Father's projects for elevating the islands, but Blaine put up his own money to finance the construction."

"I suppose it's none of my business, but I'm curious about why Blaine had, well, everything, while you . . ." My voice trailed off and the sound of the surf crashed in its wake.

"If you're thinking I've been mistreated, forget it." Ward smiled. "Father and I've had a serious misunderstanding, and he thinks I've repudiated home and country, but there's a white coral-rock villa outside Lahiana on Maui waiting for me whenever I want it."

"And you dislike it?" I asked. "You prefer Hale Malani?"

"The Maui property is closed," Ward said. "I came to Kauai because Blaine invited me, because there was this job, and because he had a piano where I could work undisturbed."

"It sounds as if you and Blaine had little in common."

"Blaine was a traditional descendant of a missionary family, but I avoid the business world. Since I'm bucking tradition, I feel duty bound to support myself and finance my education. Blaine did his best to promote Hawaii's interests, and I'll do likewise in my own way."

"Through music, you mean?"

"Right. I'm working at the Royal Poinciana because I need tuition money. I'm determined to earn a doctorate in composition. That's why this suite I'm composing is so important to me — it has to be good. If it's worthless and prosaic, then I may be forced to admit that my father was right, that I've been a fool throwing my life away."

Ward's frankness mocked my suspicions of him. He was so straightforward that the thought of his toying with yellow ginger and oblique warnings was absurd. Murder? No. If Ward had desired my departure, he would probably have bought my ticket, driven me to the airport, and personally helped me into the plane.

We had driven to the main entrance of the hotel before I realized where I was. Mammoth bulldozers and cranes all but eclipsed the Royal Poinciana trees which spangled the warm evening with their flame-tipped branches. Weblike, a painter's scaffolding veneered the facade of the structure. As we drove to the employees' parking area, I noticed the thick drop cords that snaked across the lawn to provide lighting at the dining terrace and around the oval-shaped pool where petals from the flame blossoms sequined the surface of the water.

"We're just in time." Ward jumped from

the car and helped me to a circular bench which ringed a royal palm like a starched collar. He squinted at his watch. "You may have to rush into your costume, but you must see this."

I felt gooseflesh rise on my arms as a low keening floated across the hotel grounds, magnifying the sound of the surf in the hollow seconds that followed.

"There he is." Ward nodded toward a dark-skinned boy garbed only in a plumeria lei and a short vermilion hip sarong, who was holding a giant pink and ivory shell to his lips.

"The sounding of the conch signals the torch lighting," Ward said.

The conch wailed again, and an answering call mourned like a lament. As the sounds reverberated in the flower-scented evening, another boy appeared carrying a scepterlike stave whose flaming head sent light darting into the shadows.

Strolling barefoot along the rim of the dining lanai, he ignited torches staked in threes, then he continued spreading light down a beach path. I was almost hypnotized when Ward urged me to my feet and handed me my crutches. I followed him to a small dressing room.

"Here's your costume." Ward brandished a wisp of green and gold sequined net. "I'll call a girl to help you dress, and I'll expect you out front in fifteen minutes."

Ward glanced at his watch as if intending to synchronize it with mine, then, seeing that I wore no timepiece, he shook his head and warned, "Be on time."

I was slipping from my sheath when a pretty dark-haired girl wearing an electric-blue holomuu joined me. The top of her head reached barely to my shoulder, and I was painfully aware of my height and ample proportions.

"Miss Ardan, I am Lelani. Mr. Ward directs me to help you."

"Do I ever need you, Lelani! How do I manage this outfit?"

Lelani's diminutive size and fragile beauty belied hidden strength. She helped me onto a bench, gently inserted my feet into the scant opening of the mermaid tail fin, then began zippering. Made of a stretchy fabric, the costume clung to me like Saran Wrap, and when Lelani finished, I gleamed and scintillated. But I couldn't move.

"Don't worry, Miss Ardan. Mr. Ward thinks of everything." Lelani shoved a contrivance toward me that was a wheelchair disguised to represent a lava rock and designed so I could recline in its depths.

As I curled into the chair, Lelani stood back

and clapped her hands like a delighted child. "It is true, Miss Ardan. You look like a mermaid resting on the rocks." Without another word Lelani wheeled me like a hospital patient from the dressing room to the piano. A green spotlight momentarily blinded me, but as silence descended over the dining guests, I put on my practiced smile and listened to Ward's introduction.

When my eyes adjusted to the lighting, I looked at the guests. Casually but elegantly dressed, the hotel patrons added splashes of color to the exotic scene — the men with their gay shirts and the ladies in their brightly flowered island costumes. The spicy fragrance of carnations and the sweeter aromas of pikake and plumeria masked all cooking odors, and I gazed on a scene reminiscent of a garden party.

After an elaborate arpeggio, Ward modulated into one of the songs we had rehearsed. Mercifully free of stage fright, I sang the number as we had practiced it at Hale Malani, and we responded to the crowd's applause with a second selection. Following "Blue Hawaii" with the introduction to "I'm a Palm Tree," Ward paused, turned his narrowed gaze on the audience, and invited them to sing along with us.

Wheeling me to a table away from the

spotlight at intermission time, Ward ordered black coffee, and we relaxed while we watched some young girls clad in green ti-leaf skirts perform a graceful hula to guitar accompaniment. This job was for me! It was hardly work, just fun, and the audience enjoyed these facile melodies more than if I'd knocked myself out to perform some difficult art song or operatic aria. If I could have forgotten Nona Ying and the ginger lei, the evening would have been perfect.

The last half of our work shift passed as smoothly as the first half until Liho Kalaka appeared to congratulate me. Instinctively I was on guard. Liho looked like a svelte, healthy animal in his tailored slacks and tawny silk sport shirt. Was he a murderer? Could I disguise my suspicions?

"You sing mo' bettah than other wahines." Liho winked broadly. "You the mos', Miss Ginny, ma'am."

"Why thank you, Liho. It's fun working here."

"It's robbery." Liho smirked. "Here they pay me for entertaining pretty wahines on the surfboard. For this they pay money!"

I couldn't be sure whether Liho's tone was sincere or sarcastic.

"Hawaii's an exotic and lovely state," I said.

"Especially by moonlight." Liho glanced at

the moon as if he had personally placed it for my enjoyment. "Let me drive you home. I know a route that'll take hours." His voice was low and intimate.

"I brought Miss Ardan and I'll see her home. She needs her rest if she's to work these late hours."

I glanced up in surprise at the flintiness in Ward's tone. I had had no intention of accepting Liho's arrogant invitation, but Ward's attitude infuriated me. I was about to inform him that I would go home with whom I chose when Liho surprisingly retracted his invitation.

"Forgive me, Ginny. You're so lovely that I forgot about your ankle. I know you're tired now, but perhaps you'll ride with me another time. Tomorrow? I'll show you Marlin Point by moonlight."

"All right, Liho, tomorrow. I'll look forward to it." At first I didn't realize that I had accepted a date. Seconds before, I had intended to refuse Liho; my acceptance surprised and frightened me. Ward was glowering like an angry general, so I darted Liho my brightest smile to show Ward that he couldn't order my life.

Liho took the pink plumeria lei from his neck, slipped it over my head, then brushed my cheek with a whisper of a kiss. As he walked away, he flung Ward a sardonic smile.

I wanted no involvement with Liho — with anybody. I had come to Hawaii to avoid that very thing. Liho frightened me, and his manner repelled me. He might be a murderer. Tomorrow I would break our date even if I had to walk home from work.

Ward was right. I needed rest, but I was furious at him for being so despotic as to tell me so, and, strangely, it only added to my ire to realize that his interest in me was purely professional. If anything happened to his hotel replacement, he might be delayed in leaving for the mainland. At least Liho made me feel feminine and attractive.

CHAPTER NINE

The road to the villa curved with the shore-line, and moonlight turned the waves into masses of hammered glass that shattered into shards as they smashed against the shore. My anger rose with each breaker as Ward and I drove along, separated by a silence that threatened to explode at any moment.

My nerves were raw, my ankle throbbed, and Ward's high-handed manner of managing my affairs enraged me. I needed to speak out, but I knew that if I tried, my anger would turn into sobs.

"I don't blame you for being upset." Ward's tone was neutral.

"How could you! My private life is absolutely none of your concern."

"I hate to see you fall for Liho. Don't equate good looks with good intentions."

"I'm falling for no one." I edged away from Ward, widening the isthmus of car seat between us. "But it would be none of your affair if I were. And why your sudden interest in

Liho? This afternoon you had little enough to say about him."

"And you were asking, weren't you?" Ward looked straight ahead. "You must have some mental reservations about him."

"Perhaps." I remembered Nona Ying. I remembered the yellow lei with its anonymous card.

"Well, so have I." Ward spoke sotto voce as if someone might overhear us even as we rode in the privacy of the car. "Liho's a lazy good-for-nothing with delusions of grandeur, yet he always has money to support his royal tastes."

"He earns a salary from the hotel, doesn't he?" I asked.

"I suppose." Ward sighed. "But it would take more than a few surfing lessons and catamaran sails to support him. How do you think he pays for that expensive sports car, that beach cottage, and all those clothes?"

"How do *you* think he pays for them?" I smiled as I took my turn at parrying question for question.

"I'm not sure. I can prove nothing, but I suspect that Liho's a spy."

"You're joking! What is there to spy on?"

"I think he's trying to steal information about Blaine's pineapple experiments. Blaine wanted the information to go to the research bureau, but unscrupulous persons might pay well for the data and use it for personal gain."

"I hadn't thought of that," I said. "I suppose it's possible."

"Once Blaine was gone, Liho appeared on the scene all too quickly to volunteer his services to Delores."

"If you'd offered to supervise Davao, that would have erased Liho from the picture, wouldn't it?"

Ward ignored me, and his silence made me wonder if I had accidentally stumbled upon something. Surely his supervising Davao would have been an easy solution to the problem if he really thought Liho was plotting anything underhanded.

It seemed to me that Ward was going out of his way to cast a net of suspicion around Liho, but I said nothing, remembering that I too had had the strong impression that Liho was trying to learn the safe combination on my first night at Hale Malani.

Perhaps Delores had turned to Liho for help in order to thwart Ward. Perhaps he had driven her to accept Liho's favors as he had driven me to accept an unwanted date. Pindora and Ward both warned me against Liho, but I felt a familiar determination to prove my own worth; I needed to find out about him for myself. I had no evidence that he had sent the ominous yellow lei, but I was curious as to why he had tried to hide his presence on Bette Swanson's path the night that I arrived at the villa. I felt sure that he'd dashed back to his own cottage long enough to throw another shirt on over the vivid orange one that I had seen. Pindora had said that Liho had too many women, but I doubted that Bette Swanson was one of them. I couldn't imagine the handsome Liho preening for a brassy, aging woman.

We drove on to the villa in silence, and after Ward helped me from the car, he astonished me by picking me up like a child and carrying me toward the house.

"Put me down!" I struggled, surprised at his strength.

"Hush! You'd wake Delores clattering about with those crutches." Ward walked up the stairs as if I were light as a piece of sheet music, deposited me on my bed, and promised to bring my crutches so they would be handy the following day.

I slept fitfully. In nightmares I now wore a ginger lei, and the laughter of the crowd was louder. It was almost daylight before I fell into a sound sleep. At lunchtime Delores awakened me.

"Going to nap all day?"

"Why didn't you call me earlier?" I yawned and blinked.

"Why should I disturb you?" Delores opened the draperies, and the sea breeze molded her cloud-gray shift to her body. "I want you to enjoy your visit here and to stay forever."

"I may do just that, then you'll be sorry." Although my ankle was much better, I let Delores help me into one of my muumuus. I refrained from burdening her with my suspicions about Nona Ying's accidental death; perhaps I was wrong.

"How did your first night go?" Delores asked.

"It was great, Dee. No problems at all. This is a dream setup. I've never been so pampered."

Ward's door was closed as we passed by on our way downstairs, and he was thumping out a melody.

"The maestro joining us?" I asked.

Delores shook her head. "He represented the Malanis at Nona Ying's funeral this morning, and now Pindora's fixed him a tray so he can work while he eats."

"You didn't tell me the funeral was this morning," I said.

Dee searched my face with her eyes. "It never occurred to me that you'd want to attend. Nona was such a casual acquaintance. I'm sorry. Had I known . . ."

"That's all right, Dee." It grieved me to have missed the services for Nona, but I made no issue of it. Delores had had enough sadness in the past weeks and she had no way of knowing my feelings about Nona. In a horrifying way I almost felt responsible for her death, and I felt sure her murderer would have attended the services. Murderer? Yes. I would never be convinced that her death was accidental.

"We'll eat on the side lanai today," Delores said, as if eager to turn the conversation from Nona. "It's still shaded, and you'll have an excellent view of the ocean."

After serving generous plates of chop suey along with frosted glasses of lime and mint ade, Pindora hovered over us until Delores asked her to leave. We enjoyed a leisurely meal, and as I finished eating, I noticed that the amakua god on the balcony above us still wore a wilted ginger lei. The sight of the withered blossoms brought back memories of my nightmares, and I remembered the warning message, Nona Ying, and the disturbing letter that Delores had written to me and then destroyed.

No one was near, yet I spoke in a hushed voice. "Delores, surely you can tell me what it was that upset you so much before I arrived here. It's unlike you to hide from a difficult situation. Remember, I came to help, to be useful."

"Do you sense danger?" Delores stared toward the mountains, and I knew without looking that a storm brewed in that high rain forest. It was reflected in her face, her voice.

"No, I sense nothing," I lied, hoping my words would comfort her. I couldn't risk upsetting her by telling the truth. "What's bothering you?"

"I know that it's nothing," Delores said. "At first I refused to believe that Blaine, my Blaine, could have had an accident, especially a — a fatal accident. I made a fool of myself, but the police finally convinced me that they were right." Delores' voice was brittle, and I knew that she, in turn, was lying to me, trying to spare me from something.

"And Dr. Niilonu has helped me," she continued. "He explained that I was overcome with grief and that facing reality at a time like this is often difficult. But he's helped me. I shouldn't have written in such a panic to you, but I was selfish enough to want you to keep me company. Ginny, whatever am I going to do here all alone?"

I seized the opportunity I'd been waiting for. "Let's go back to the mainland, Dee. We'll find interesting jobs somewhere and make new lives for ourselves."

Delores walked to the edge of the patio, then stood facing me with her knees stiffened in that stubborn way I remembered so well. "I must stay, Ginny. At least for a while. For Blaine's sake I must see the pineapple experiments to completion."

I shifted my ankle to a more comfortable position and forced myself to avoid the argument I was sure to lose. "Then remain you must, and I'll stick with you." Delores was keeping something back from me, and I was afraid I knew what it was. I had the unpleasant suspicion that she was much more attracted to Liho Kalaka than to pineapple experiments. Liho seemed to be the only person who could pierce the tranquilizer-induced state in which she existed.

I felt guilty as I remembered my promise to see Liho after work that night. Although I had no intention of hurting Delores, I was suddenly determined to keep this date I'd made in haste and high anger. Liho and I needed to have an understanding about Delores. Perhaps Ward was right in thinking that Liho was trying to pirate the experimental data, but I doubted it. Delores was a wealthy woman, and I didn't intend to sit by and let her fling herself at a man who was interested only in her money.

As the sun inched across the sky, the

shadow of the amakua image fell like a dark blot across the lanai, and, staring up at the ugly, leering face, I didn't see Liho until his arrogant voice rumbled a greeting and he swaggered across the flagstones to a chair.

"Aloha, ladies. I come to help Davao grow bigger and better pines for the glory of the islands."

"Davao's already out in the beds, Liho." Delores said his name with an intimate, personal lilt.

"You have one great sistah, Miss Delores." Liho assumed a heavy accent. "She gif the haoles the wow las' night."

"I can imagine." Delores smiled at me. "I'd like to have seen you in that mermaid costume."

"Then come along tonight," I invited. I hoped Liho would echo my invitation; I was eager to get Delores circulating in society again. The sooner she was able to face a normal life, the sooner she could discard the tranquilizers. But Liho only voiced the thought that was mirrored all too clearly in my sister's eyes.

"Delores needs seclusion, Ginny." Then he tilted his shaggy head. "Besides, I'm a jealous man. Tonight I want you to myself. You will sing only for me."

Liho spoke with the air of a male completely sure of the admiration of two women, then without waiting for comment, he glided through the Pandanus grove and on to the pineapple beds.

"Don't let Liho smooth talk you with all that sweet sounding pidgin." Delores spoke with real concern in her voice.

"Relax, Dee. I'm a bastion of unsusceptibility where beach boy kings are concerned." I tried to help Delores clear the table, but she insisted that I rest on the lounge chair in the warm shade. As I leaned back against the cushions, I saw a blue pleasure boat a short distance from shore. Brightly dressed figures crowded the boat rail, and I guessed that their guide must be pointing out the carved figure that rested on the balcony above me. I watched until the boat diminished to a black hyphenlike speck on the horizon, then I scanned the newspaper that Delores dropped into my lap.

I didn't intend to nap, but I knew I had slept a long time when I awakened and found Delores in the kitchen preparing sukiyaki. She informed me that Pindora and Davao had gone to the village for supplies. As Ward came into the kitchen I rested my crutches against the refrigerator and tested my weight on my injured ankle.

"None of that." Ward pulled up a kitchen

stool for me. "Let that ankle heal completely before you start using it again. The Royal Poinciana guests are going to want to see you in something besides that mermaid costume before long."

"I should have known your concern was purely of a business nature." The waspishness in my voice surprised me, and I tried to soften the rest of my words. "But never fear, I'm no stoic. My ankle feels better, and I'm sure I'll be walking soon."

Dinner was a grim affair despite Delores' excellent cooking. Although Ward never mentioned Liho's driving me home, I sensed his disapproval.

I begged Delores to come with us to the Royal Poinciana, but she refused and Ward did nothing to try to change her mind. We drove to the hotel in silence. Although we arrived in time to hear the conches wailing in the still evening, Ward didn't pause to listen. He marched toward the dining terrace, and in a few moments Lelani came to help me dress.

"Lelani, what a lovely name you have. It's like silvery moonlight and pink plumeria." I paused in admiration.

"Lelani was the name of an island princess of long ago," Lelani said. "My Hawaiian mother named me. Her name is Naniluu."

"You're on!" Ward's drill sergeant command rang out before I had finished applying my makeup, but Lelani was unperturbed. She was much like a princess; she possessed an age-old Polynesian beauty and enough dignity to become any person of royal blood.

Ward and I performed our first set of three songs to an enthusiastic crowd, and the evening that at first had promised to be a grueling ordeal gradually burgeoned into one of relaxed enjoyment.

Liho was reigning over a group of teenagers, and the girls watching him reminded me of famished children staring into a bakery display case. Liho basked in the golden warmth of their attentions, but I noticed his obsidian eyes frequently dart in my direction.

I was looking forward to the moonlight ride home with mixed feelings of anticipation and dread. I had no fear for my physical safety. If Liho were the one trying to get rid of me, he surely wouldn't dare act tonight, not with Ward fully aware of our plans. I'd had so little experience in dating and in trying to understand men that I felt like a first grader confronted with a problem in algebra. Yet this was no real date by any means; I only intended to give Liho Kalaka a few of my thoughts concerning Delores and to let Ward know that I was independent of him.

When the evening ended, Ward packed microphones, spotlights, and music, and by the time I'd dressed and was at last in Liho's gold-toned sports car, Ward had disappeared. I smiled, remembering the narrow winding road to Hale Malani; Ward would hardly care to follow. He had undoubtedly hurried to get a head start.

With a slight frown at the crutches thrusting awkwardly between us, Liho swung onto the black leather seat like a monarch preparing to show off the royal coach. But when he turned the crested key in the ignition, the car refused to start. Muttering Hawaiian expletives unlisted in the tourist's handy phrase book, Liho flung open the trunk lid and I heard metallic clanging and banging.

After some fifteen minutes of frenetic effort Liho persuaded the motor to cooperate, and the force of our jetlike takeoff molded me to the upholstery. I sat with my eyes shut listening to the roar of the wind and feeling it sting my face and whip my hair. Once on the main road Liho slowed down, and as I regained my composure, he scrutinized the dark roadside groves of palms.

"I promised you Marlin Point." Liho's voice boiled with excitement. "Feel up to it?"

"Of course, but brief me first. Is there a legend?"

"No legend." Liho slowed the car to a crawl

as he turned onto a rutted lane leading toward the shimmering ocean. We jogged a few yards over the bumpy terrain, then he braked to a stop.

"Let's walk to the point," Liho invited. "Can you make it if I help you?" Liho opened my door and pulled out my crutches. "Years ago my great-grandfather told of coming here and seeing marlin playing in the open sea. I can't promise you any leaping fish tonight, but there is a blowhole in the ledge underneath the lookout point. It's smaller than the ones on the tourist trails, but it's well worth seeing."

I knew that a blowhole was an opening in the lava rock shelf where waves rushed under and splashed water up through the aperture with such force that it formed a spouting geyser of brine. I hobbled along beside Liho, planning how I would steer the conversation to Delores once I had viewed this wonder of nature. For once I welcomed my crutches; surely they would thwart any amorous inclinations on Liho's part.

Reaching a black platform of rocks that jutted into the ocean, I inched more cautiously over the slippery surface. The pungent smell of sea life filled the air, and a cool mist sprayed my cheeks which were warm from the exertion of my clumsy walking. I tasted salt spray as I stood enthralled by the mass of water which whipped into a meringue. Liho left me, walked farther on, then called over his shoulder.

"I can see the blowhole from here, Ginny. Let me help you."

Suddenly I was afraid. I'd been a fool to come here. My desire to "show" Ward and to protect Delores had betrayed me. I wanted to escape. But I was helpless, and I was too proud to let Liho suspect my weakness. Taking my right crutch, he offered me his left arm, and as we walked to the edge of the rocks, he shouted above the roar of the sea.

"Ginny, lean a bit to your left." He pointed to the blowhole.

I leaned toward the ocean, and in that split instant Liho pushed me. I heard myself scream as I fought to regain my balance, and the next moment I catapulted into the churning water. Although I am a strong swimmer, the relentless waves pounded me against the protruding lava rock like a limp reed. The current dragged me down, down into oblivion. I struggled. I choked.

CHAPTER TEN

The next moments were a living nightmare. The razor-sharp coral and the abrasive lava rock lacerated my skin while the cold salt water stung my wounds. The taste of brine and the grit of sand filled my mouth, and the living-fish smell of the sea permeated my whole being.

I fought. I fought until strength left me, then, exhausted, I surrendered. I thought I was dying — that this overwhelming helplessness was the beginning of death itself. But I know now that I merely blacked out for a few minutes.

I heard water boiling around me for some time before I found strength to open my eyes. Only then did I realize that I was not in the seething sea, but instead was resting on submerged rock where waves still sloshed over me. As I groaned and tried to turn my head, a warm hand closed on my shoulder and I heard Ward's voice.

"Easy, Ginny, and hush. Everything'll be

okay." Ward's soothing words failed to assuage my fears, and I sat up choking and spluttering while pain and nausea tried to pound me back into a prone position.

"Where . . . where am I? What are you d-doing here?" I was vaguely conscious that my head was in Ward's lap and that he was as waterlogged as I.

"Keep calm, Ginny. We're on a narrow lava ledge under Marlin Point. How do you feel? How's your ankle?"

"Liho pushed me!" My voice shrilled to a siren scream as I relived the horrible moment. "He tried to drown me!"

"Hush!" Ward covered my mouth with a wet, salty palm and spoke with his head so close to mine that I felt his breath warm my ear. "Liho's gone now, but he'll be back."

"How do you know? What are you doing here?"

"He'll return because some eerie force always entices a murderer back to the scene of his crime. He'll have to satisfy himself that you didn't survive the fall, and if we're quiet, he may think he accomplished his mission. At any rate, we must stay hidden."

"But what'll we do?"

"If Liho does discover us down here, perhaps the surprise will throw him off guard and give me a chance to strike the first blow.

How do you feel?"

"Terrible."

"Any broken bones?"

"All of them. What *were* you doing here?" Now that I felt well enough to complain, questions soared like hungry gulls in my mind.

"I was checking up on you." Easing me to a sitting position, Ward supported me against his chest and shoulder, and my hand touched a soaking coil of rope that he must have used in his rescue.

Ward continued, "That card which arrived with the ginger lei fell from your pocket when you leaned over to pick up your crutches. After reading it, I knew you were in danger. I tried to tell you about Liho last night. I'd have made my warning clearer if I hadn't thought you'd tell Delores. I didn't want her upset again."

"So you followed us?" Chills numbed me as I tried to fit the puzzle together, and at the same time I wondered how a person thanked someone for saving her life.

"Last night I heard Liho mention Marlin Point, so I arrived first, hid my car, and sneaked down here ready to help you if you needed me."

"You suspected that Liho was . . ."

"I suspect a lot of things that I can't prove.

Maybe now you'll help me — if you're not afraid."

"I'm scared to death!" I cried. "Liho can't get away with this, can he?" I thought of Blaine, of Nona Ying.

Before Ward could answer we heard car doors slam above the roar of the ocean. Ward pulled me against him and we flattened ourselves against the back of the ledge. Pure terror erased my pain. If Liho discovered us huddled here, we were lost. Ward was no physical match for Liho.

Several voices rose in excited shouts. It took me a moment to realize that Liho wasn't alone, but the clamor galvanized Ward into action. I wished I could have seen Liho's face when he realized that I was safe; it might have spared me much soul-searching in the days to come. But I didn't, and he had ample time to mask his feelings in the moments between Ward's first call and the actual appearance of our rescuers.

Liho, Dr. Niilonu, and a hospital aide helped Ward and me to safety. Liho was full of apologies as they carried me on a stretcher to the ambulance for the ride to the hospital.

"It was my fault," Liho said. "I pushed you. I slipped, and I accidentally shoved you into the ocean. I knew my only chance to save you was to go for help. Thank goodness the hospital was nearby."

"It would have been more practical to have pulled her from the water before you sought help," Ward said.

"I know the riptides and undertows that slice around this point," Liho said. "I had no hope of rescuing her alone."

"Mr. Malani seems to have managed it." Moonlight etched deep shadows into Dr. Niilonu's craggy face as he gazed at Ward's sodden, grimy clothing. "It was lucky that you happened along when you did, Ward."

"Only a fool would have braved those waters," Liho blustered. "I grew up in that ocean; I know it like my own backyard."

I waited for Ward to admit that he had been hiding, well prepared for a rescue, but he merely shrugged. Liho with all his muscles and medals was confounded.

Dr. Niilonu insisted that I spend the next few days in the hospital. Luckily, I had no fractures, but I was so bruised and battered that I welcomed the chance to rest and recover.

Ward went home and returned with Delores before I slept, and if my sister thought my fall anything but accidental, she pretended otherwise. Once assured that I was only superficially injured, she let Ward take her back home.

When I opened my eyes the next morning, I was surprised to see Pindora flitting about my hospital room and pleased to find the sweet fragrance of flowers battling more prosaic antiseptic odors. Noticing that I had awakened, Pindora brought a flaming bouquet of red hibiscus to my bedside. Although every muscle protested, I reached for the card and read, "Aloha, with most sincere apologies, Liho."

Sleep had erased some of the previous night's horror, and now, in this safe place, I began to wonder if Ward and I had been wrong — to wonder if the whole dreadful affair hadn't been accidental.

Without showing Pindora the message, I dropped the card in among the crimson blossoms. "Pindora, how nice of you to come visit me."

"It is a pleasure as well as a duty, Missy." Pindora cranked up the head of my bed and offered me a drink. "Mr. Ward insists that I stay with you every minute you are here."

"Pindora! That's absurd! I'm perfectly all right. Dr. Niilonu is only keeping me here for a rest. In a few days even my ankle will be healed."

"Mr. Ward orders me to keep daytime guard." Pindora patted a wayward strand of dark fringe that jutted from her forehead like an antenna. "Davao sits outside your door all night."

The thought of the taciturn, disdainful Hawaiian sitting owllike by my hospital door unnerved me almost as much as realizing that Ward believed that I was in real danger and had taken efficient measures to protect me. Pindora must have guessed my thoughts.

"You — your mishap, Missy. It was an accident? You are sure?"

"Of course it was an accident, Pindora. How is Ward explaining this round-the-clock guard to Delores? I hope he hasn't frightened her with his suspicions."

"Mr. Ward tells your sister the same thing that he tells Davao and me. He says we are here to relieve the regular nurses and to see that you have every attention."

I was confused. Liho had behaved as if my fall had been accidental, had publicly assumed the blame, and had rushed for help. I could think of no real reason why he would want to be rid of me, and for the sake of my sanity, I tried to accept his account of the previous night. At least until I had time and strength to search out answers to the multitude of questions that plagued me.

Dr. Niilonu allowed me no visitors on my first day in the hospital, and I was glad. I felt as if I had slept on a bed of nails, and now a small man inside my head beat on a tambourine while his helper encased all my muscles in iron bands.

Beginning with my second day in the hospital, Liho visited me morning and afternoon, padding about the tiny room like a huge caged beast, but Pindora gave us no privacy. Liho was all remorse and solicitude, and my room became so filled with his floral offerings that I had many of the plants and bouquets distributed to other patients.

Ward and Delores also visited me, and although Delores never seemed to doubt that my fall had been accidental, Ward behaved as if he were personally responsible for the life he had saved, and he refused to lift the guard on my room.

Ward's concern for me was touching, and I sensed a warmth in him that had been absent before my fall. He also stopped by each evening before work, and I looked forward to his visits with more anticipation than I cared to admit. Although I had a host of questions to ask Ward, Pindora never left us alone, and I was too proud to ask her to leave the room and thus risk having Ward think I was using my questions as a ruse to enable me to be alone with him.

When Dr. Niilonu stopped by on my fourth

morning in the hospital, he found me more amiable than usual. Although my bruised arms and legs still looked like avant-garde abstractions in yellowish purple, I was able to walk without crutches. The doctor smiled, then studied his charts and records.

"I believe you can go home this afternoon, Miss Ardan. Are you ready to leave?"

"Ready and eager, Doctor. I only wish I could go this morning and arrive at the villa in time for lunch on the lanai."

"The hospital meals are barely tolerable, aren't they?" Dr. Niilonu sighed. "My regular cook and dietitian is visiting her mother on the mainland, and I'm operating with substitute help. Don't know what I'll do if Mrs. Napalouma doesn't return soon."

"Are you serious?" I asked.

"Certainly," Dr. Niilonu said. "Right now, I'm personally making menus and begging a neighbor to pinch-hit as cook."

"You might ask Delores to help you out," I said. "She's a terrific cook, and she needs something to do. A responsibility might help her to readjust her life."

"I didn't know your sister liked to cook," Dr. Niilonu replied. "Of course she has no financial need of a job. I might offend her by suggesting such a thing."

"With your permission I'll ask her myself,

Doctor. Delores needs something worthwhile to do."

"You're right, Miss Ardan. I'll speak to her about this when she comes for you this afternoon." Dr. Niilonu left, and while Pindora packed my things, I called Delores and told her of my discharge. Pindora and I spent the rest of the morning distributing Liho's flowers to other patients. Never before having received flowers from a man, I decided, against Pindora's wishes, to keep one permanent arrangement which fascinated me. A white ceramic whale's tooth held black sand from Hawaii, fernlike black coral from Mauai, and small, stubby fingers of white coral from Oahu's shores. It was a study in contrasts that to me epitomized the whole Hawaiian scene.

When Delores arrived after lunch, I sensed her excitement, and I knew before she spoke that Dr. Niilonu had made his request and that she had accepted. Some of the old spark had returned to her eyes. Pindora's cheeks flushed with pleasure, and I knew she was thinking of being undisputed queen in the Hale Malani kitchen.

"If it's all right, I'll let Davao drive you home, Ginny. I want to check the kitchen equipment and the supplies, and Dr. Niilonu has asked for help with tomorrow's menu." Delores saw Pindora and me to the limousine and helped arrange my things on the back seat.

"Ward wanted to come with us this afternoon, but . . ." Her voice trailed off, and I wondered what she had almost said, but I was so eager to leave the hospital that I didn't pursue the subject. Davao drove to Hale Malani in his usual brooding silence, but Pindora chattered at him until we stopped at the front entrance.

Once again the somberness of the villa chilled me, and I sensed that the brown lava-rock facade masked secrets that I needed to discover if Delores and I were to continue living here.

I had expected Ward to say hello, but although we made all sorts of noise in the hallway outside his door, he never appeared. A minor melody flowed from his piano uninterrupted.

As I stretched out on my bed to rest, I tried to forget Ward, but he crashed into my thoughts uninvited. Perhaps it was only natural to react strongly toward someone who had thought me worthy enough to risk his life for. Yet I knew my feeling for Ward was more than gratitude. I remembered his strong arms as he carried me up the stairs, the gentle touch of his hand as we listened to the sounding of the conches, and the warmth of his body as he protected me on the ledge at Marlin Point. Suddenly I was afraid, afraid of this man who was breaking through the barrier I had thrown up between me and all men.

Inner voices harangued me to break through my domino wall, to take my place in the world as a woman, but I wasn't ready. Liho may have tried to drown me, but my fear of him was like the fluttering butterflies of stage fright compared to my terror of Ward Malani and the feelings he aroused in me.

Yet for the first time I wanted to fight this fear that shadowed my life — fight it and conquer it. *You can change if you want to.* Delores' words, spoken long ago, echoed in my mind.

At first I had no idea of how to fight. I had spent a lifetime hiding myself from others. I wasn't ready to bare my soul to outsiders. At last I had the idea of keeping some sort of a journal, starting with my childhood. I would write down the story of my life. Perhaps such a private outpouring of words onto paper would be therapeutic.

I began writing that afternoon, and as I wrote I began to sense a freedom I had never known before.

CHAPTER ELEVEN

I didn't see Ward until suppertime, and by then I felt up to facing him. My heart leaped when he ordered Pindora to set a table for two on the side lanai. Somehow I managed to eat my meal and keep up my side of the conversation. Then, after Pindora whisked away our dishes, Ward grew serious.

"Are you afraid, Ginny?"

I knew he was referring to my accident. "You mean of Liho?"

Ward nodded, but before I answered, he continued. "You have reason to be afraid. Liho tried to hide his tracks by admitting that he pushed you, but don't let him fool you."

"But he did go for help," I said. "And he visited me twice a day in the hospital." I wanted to believe my fall had been accidental.

"Big deal!" Ward pounded the table with his fist. "He went for help because he knew that everyone at the hotel had seen you leaving together, and he knew that no amount of

144

aid could save you after even a few minutes in those raging waters."

"Perhaps you're right." I shuddered. "But why would Liho hate me so? And what can I do?"

"Be on guard," Ward said. "If you're brave enough to stick it out here, to pretend to everyone that you do think Liho accidentally shoved you, we may be able to trap him."

I had a choice. Yesterday I would have run for the mainland, but today my writing had given me new strength. I was still not a whole person, but I was ridding myself of a terrible sickness. I felt sure of that, so sure that I refused to run. I would forget personal fears. I would consider Delores. Now I knew for sure that her letter had been sincere. Something sinister lurked just out of sight, some evil that had to be met sooner or later. Ward interpreted my silence as indecision.

"We have one advantage that perhaps you've overlooked."

"What's that?" I asked.

"We know for sure who our enemy is. Up until your fall I had just been guessing. Even Nona Ying's death in no way pointed to Liho."

"I've felt all along that Nona was murdered," I said. "Do you believe that too?"

"Yes, but I can find no motive."

"The murderer mistook her for me," I said.

"I'm positive. We were dressed similarly that night, and — and I'd even lent Nona my turban. I feel — responsible. But I have no proof. We can't go to the police with flimsy suppositions."

"Thank goodness you understand that." Ward flashed me a smile. "Delores never could understand. She suspected that Blaine was murdered, and she wanted the police to act immediately."

"You disagreed?"

"I knew Blaine well enough to doubt that he had a foolish accident. But proving murder is difficult. Blaine's personality was as bland as vanilla custard; he had no enemies. Several circumstantial matters pointed to Liho, but I kept quiet. Even if he had been indicted, I felt sure that any jury would free him. And a person acquitted of a crime can't be tried again for that same offense. I want Liho brought to court only when we have a sure case against him."

"So that's why Delores felt that you had turned against her."

"She told you that?" Ward frowned.

"She wrote it in a letter. She's never mentioned it since."

Ward shrugged. "Who can blame her? I've kept my suspicions of Liho to myself."

"Why?"

"I was afraid Delores might refuse his help in managing Davao."

"That makes no sense," I said.

"I refused to supervise Davao because I wanted Liho here — here where I could watch him. I wanted to give him a chance to trap himself."

"I think your scheme's backfired. Delores has fallen in love with him."

"I hope not," Ward said. "She's stronger than she was. She realized she was nearing a breakdown; she went to the doctor of her own accord. He has helped her, calmed her to the point where she can accept reason."

"I think the pills have only masked her troubles," I said. "But what do you intend to do? You're going to leave here soon."

"Much can happen in a short time. Liho will betray himself sooner or later. If it isn't sooner, then I advise both you and Delores to leave Kauai. You have no valid reason for staying, and I'll return later to deal with Liho."

In spite of my writing and my new insights, my old feelings of inadequacy washed over me again. I shuddered. Kauai had proved to be anything but the sanctuary I searched for. If we found no solid proof against Liho within the next few days, I would not only have to return to the mainland, but I would also have to persuade Delores to go with me. The villa would be unsafe for her without Ward's presence.

"I hate this whole affair as badly as you do," Ward said. "But perhaps we'll work out a solution; I have a few plans in the back of my mind. Promise me you'll be on guard, Ginny. Promise that you'll avoid the beach."

"Ward! I'll go crazy here with nothing to do except worry."

"Then promise that you'll swim only when Liho's at the Royal Poinciana. I want you to tell me whenever you leave the villa."

I nodded.

After Ward left for the hotel, I sat alone. I welcomed his concern, and for the first time I felt that I was more to him than just a business partner, a co-worker. He made me feel safe and cherished, yet I was still frightened of the strange feelings astir within me.

Again I began writing, setting on paper all the fears that had forced me to withdraw from life. I don't know whether it was the writing or the fact that for the first time in my life I was taking a positive action in my own behalf, but something gave me strength and staying power.

I even began telling myself that I was a worthwhile individual. I wrote those very words down on paper, and I repeated them so often that they began to seem like the truth.

In the next days I made a habit of relaxing on the lanai during the morning when Liho worked with Davao. Liho always spoke casually, and I answered in kind, assured that Ward was nearby and alert for danger.

Time at the villa flowed smoothly as sand through an hour glass. With Delores occupied at the hospital, quarrels between her and Pindora ended; Ward worked ceaselessly at his composition; and I spent long, restful hours soaking up sunshine and writing about all the things that had ever bothered me.

Ward had not suggested that I return to work, but I was ready. Now that I was off crutches, I wanted to tackle all the fears that loomed like specters ready to defeat me. I wanted to see Liho in safe, well-populated surroundings. I wanted to watch him, to circumspectly study his behavior, to search every aspect of his demeanor for the flaw that would snare him. Time melted away, and I had to do something — to think of some way to prevent us from having to leave Kauai.

On the third morning after my release from the hospital, the storms that usually battled in the mountains deluged the island. I gave up my writing in favor of finishing repairs on Bette Swanson's scrapbooks.

After lunch, I usually took a sunbath and

wrote for an hour or so, but today I decided to return the books to Bette Swanson. Then, if there was time, I would swim. I took the public lane to the beach and approached the cottage from the front. The air was still steamy, but the rain had retreated to the mountains.

At first I thought I was imagining things. Surf pounding sand sometimes creates strange illusions, but as the waves receded, I heard two voices rise in anger. Bette Swanson's brassy soprano capped more subdued male tones. I turned to retreat, but Pele noticed me. The Pekingese set up a volley of barking, and I almost dropped the scrapbooks in my haste to pat her and remind her that we had met before.

After Pele's canine fanfare, there was nothing to do but go on up to the cottage. Mentally I prepared apologies for my intrusion, but when I reached the terrace, I found Bette Swanson listening to a radio and sipping a glass of minted tea. She wore a vivid green muumuu, and in her colorful way she was a portrait of tranquility. Only a sooty smear on her cheek hinted that a tear might have passed that way.

"Hello, Miss Swanson." I smiled as I approached. "Forgive me for barging in, but I know you must be wanting your clippings."

"I wasn't worried about them." Bette Swanson controlled her clarion voice, and I heard the resonant timbre that had been world famous. But in the next instant her speech was lifeless, dull, and she flicked an imaginary ash from her cigarillo.

"Sit down and let me get you some tea."

"Thank you. I'd love some."

Bette Swanson went into the house and stayed long enough to make me wonder if some furtive caller lurked inside waiting for me to leave. But perhaps I had only imagined the voices. Bette could have been scolding Pele above the clamor of the radio. When she returned with the tea, I spoke first.

"Thank you so much." I sipped tea while she paced about the terrace. "I thoroughly enjoyed reading your scrapbooks. What a wonderful life! To have known such success must give you a great satisfaction."

"Success is an ephemeral thing," Miss Swanson said. "I held it in the palm of my hand, but suddenly it slipped through my fingers. There's no sound more hauntingly beautiful than the staccato beat of applause."

Suddenly I felt sorry for this tired woman. Did she remember her many triumphs only in terms of applause and adulation?

"Miss Swanson, I'm ready to begin lessons whenever you have time."

Bette Swanson paced back and forth across the terrace like a prima donna in a full spotlight, then she bowed her head and faced me.

"I must retract my offer. I'd like to help. Believe me, there's nothing I'd rather do, but I cannot, I must not do it at this time. Perhaps later."

The expression on Bette Swanson's face confounded me. She looked like a person walking in the black of night who had forgotten the splendor of the sun. I saw a mixture of furtiveness, hopelessness, and worst of all, self-pity, but her eyes bespoke a sadness greater than the sum of all of these.

"That's quite all right, Miss Swanson. I realize that you're in retirement — a well-deserved retirement."

"I'm truly sorry to have to refuse, Ginny, but many things are beyond my control."

Looking exhausted, literally worn out, Bette Swanson leaned her head against the chair cushion, and I seized upon the lull in our conversation to make my exit. I thanked her again for sharing her scrapbooks, but all the while I wondered if her antipathy toward Delores had influenced her decision to refrain from coaching me. She remained seated when I left, but Pele accompanied me down the beach.

Bette Swanson was an enigma. After seeing her and Delores together, I hadn't expected her to inquire as to my sister's health; it was obvious that strong feelings of animosity separated them. But I felt certain that Miss Swanson must have heard about my fall and hospitalization, yet she had not mentioned them.

I walked down the deserted beach a short distance, slipped off my robe, and splashed into the surf. The cool water felt like satin slipping over my skin, and I played in the waves. At last tired, yet inwardly rested, I slogged back to the beach and stretched out to drip-dry while I watched fragile white sand crabs skittering from one dark round hole to another. I dozed for a few minutes, and when I awakened my mouth was parched.

Shaking the sand from my robe, I tossed it over my arm, picked up my sneakers, and headed toward the villa. What eerie force is it that draws one against one's will back to a scene of horror, a scene best forgotten? I fought the impulse to revisit the spot where I had found Nona Ying that first morning on the beach. But silent voices called me, and I followed them to the area where brown lava rock burgeoned into high bluffs. Out of respect for my weak ankle, I walked carefully and kept one eye on the incoming breakers.

The tide was low, and, leaving my things on the sand, I waded waist deep around a high stony isthmus that extended like a bony finger into the sea, and I saw again the horseshoe-shaped cove where limpid water lapped against the boulders. Here in the bright sunshine it was hard to believe that this had been a pool of death.

I was leaning on a rock trying to erase the vision of Nona Ying from my mind when I noticed the low opening in the most protected area of the cove. A cave? I swam across the quiet water, ducked my head low, and peeked into utter blackness.

Diving for a seashell, I lobbed it through the opening and heard an echoing splash. Curiosity won. I swam through the aperture into a dank, musty-smelling cavern, touched my feet onto a rocky support, and stopped, afraid to venture into the darkness.

As my eyes adjusted to the murkiness, I saw that I stood at the brink of a large pool. The only light came from the low opening through which I had just passed, and I couldn't tell whether the water was deep or shallow.

This hidden spot was clammy, cold, and eerie, and I was ready to abandon it when all at once I made out a ghostly form floating in the far distance. Was it a boat? It could have been anything. Curiosity urged investigation, but gripping fingers of fear held me back. Shivering, I swam through the opening in the rocks back to the warmth and light and safety I needed.

CHAPTER TWELVE

I scrambled over the brown boulders toward the white sand. Where I had walked on dry land only moments ago, the tide now curled around my ankles. I broke into a frenzied run when I reached firm damp ground just above the surf line. As I veered toward the path to the main road, I would have crashed into Ward had he not reached out to catch me.

Once again I felt his surprising strength, but as I looked up at him, I saw a stranger. A ruddy flush flooded his cheeks, his eyes gleamed, and a wild excitement sparked his face.

"Ward! What is it?" My personal fright abated as I tried to read his countenance. Had something happened to Delores? Had she cracked under the strain of hospital routine?

"Where have you been?" Ward spoke quietly, but rough emotion grated in his tone. "You promised to tell me whenever you left the villa."

"I thought it foolish to bother you in the afternoon when we both knew Liho was at the hotel working."

"That's just it! Liho isn't at the Royal Poinciana. I telephoned a few minutes ago to check on a damaged amplifier, and Lelani mentioned that Liho had taken the afternoon off. He may be surfing — practicing for the sea carnival on Friday — or he may be lurking here. We can't afford to take chances."

Ward linked his arm through mine and strolled toward the ocean. I was conscious of his warmth, the clean smell of his skin, but my mind was on the angry voices I had heard earlier at Bette Swanson's. Perhaps Liho had been in her cottage all the while I was visiting with her on the terrace.

"Smile," Ward said. "Liho may be watching us, and I don't want him to guess that I came here to protect you. As of this minute we're merely two friends keeping a swimming date."

The thought of my being alone on this deserted beach with Liho left me weak, and when Ward dropped down onto the sand, I sat beside him without protest. He placed a warm hand over my cold one, and I made no effort to escape his touch.

"Forgive me," Ward said. "I didn't mean to frighten you like this, but when I found you gone from the villa . . ."

"It's all right," I said. "You just surprised me. I'd been visiting Bette Swanson, and when I left her I thought I was alone."

"Then why were you running? You almost knocked me down."

I hated to admit my fright, but Ward's eyes demanded an answer. "Did you know there's a cavern in that cove beyond those rocks?" I nodded in the direction from which I had just come.

"A cave? Are you sure?"

"Of course I'm sure! Kauai's your home! I'd think you'd have discovered it long ago."

"I've never spent much time here, Ginny. As a kid I had a matched set of allergies, and something at the villa aggravated them. The rest of the family spent their summers here, but for the most part I remained on Oahu with my grandmother."

"How lonely for you." I pictured a dark, wide-eyed child left behind while his brothers and sisters were off on a gay holiday.

"Save your sympathy," Ward said. "I liked to read and listen to Gram's tales about her early days on the islands. We got on admirably. But this cave, Ginny. You really found one?"

"It's near the back of that cove." Something kept me from mentioning the shadowy form inside the greenish cavern — the form

157

that might have been a boat, Blaine's boat.

"Blaine used to talk about some supersecret cave near the villa." Ward chuckled. "But I never paid too much attention to his tales. However, unexplored caves are common; they honeycomb the bluffs of the Na Pali coast. They're really lava tubes formed by gasses during volcanic eruptions."

Ward's scientific explanation of the cave didn't lessen my apprehension. "This one's eerie, Ward. That's where I'd been just before I met you. All I wanted to do was to escape — to get away from it as fast as I could."

"Did you go inside?"

I nodded, knowing that my voice would shake if I tried to describe the sensations I had felt in that dank hole.

"Many of the high cliff caves were used as burying places," Ward said. "The bones of the alii, the ancient Hawaiian royalty, along with their favorite canoes and artifacts were deposited in the lava tubes by natives who lowered the items over the rim of the cliff with sturdy ropes. See anything unusual in this cave?"

I shuddered and shook my head. A tomb! No wonder I had felt such a creepy sensation. I wondered if the floating object might have been the favorite canoe of some ancient monarch. But how ridiculous! Even if other explorers had somehow missed seeing it, no craft would survive for centuries in the water.

"Let's go back to the villa," I said.

"Not yet," Ward replied. "That would look as if I had come to take you home under guard. Relax. You're perfectly safe now. Let's walk over to your cave. I'd like to see if it's really there."

Ward stood and pulled me to my feet. Having no desire to return to the shadowy depths of the cavern, I hesitated for a moment, but Ward's presence gave me the courage that I needed.

"Okay. But let's go quickly if we must and get it over with." I started to run, but Ward put an arm around my waist and forced me to walk at his side. It was several minutes before we reached the cove. I had relaxed enough to realize that I had been foolish to have been so frightened.

Approaching the lava rock rise, I took Ward's hand for support, and we crawled over the boulders until we looked down into the quiet blue pool.

Perplexed, I scanned the vertical bluff in the arc of the shoreline. Oblique shafts of light spangled the verdure of tropical growth that grew almost to the waterline, but the black, yawning hole had disappeared.

"I don't see an opening now," I said.

"Maybe you imagined it. Many of these craggy formations might seem to lead to a cave, whereas in reality they end in shallow tonguelike niches in the embankment."

"I was inside a cavern." Stupefied, I searched the bluffs; then I remembered the rising water. "The tide! The tide's blocked the entrance; it was small enough when I was here earlier."

"Could be," Ward said. "But it's unimportant. If you found a cave, you found a cave. I believe you. Just remember that it's nothing to be frightened of. We'll come back another day and you can show it to me."

Again we climbed over the rocks back to the beach, and once more Ward pulled me down onto the sand beside him. We put on a good imitation of an infatuated couple for anyone who might be watching, and I was beginning to like our pantomime. Never before had I let myself enjoy a man's company, but now it seemed almost natural.

"The suite is coming along," Ward said. "Of course, there's work to do before it's ready to submit to the Mission Children's Society. I'll have to recopy the manuscript, and score the instrumental parts before anyone can make any sense of it. I'll leave Kauai long before those jobs are finished."

"I only feel safe while you're here, yet I

know you have to go."

"Ginny, in less than eight hours you and Delores could both be back on the mainland — back in New York, and away from this whole mess. Delores' lawyers could manage the legal angles."

I shuddered at the thought of New York. "That's no solution. Delores'll balk at leaving Kauai before the pineapple experiments are complete, and I'll never abandon her here. I want to start working at the hotel again, Ward. I've no plans for exposing Liho, but maybe my presence will goad him into some sort of action. Or maybe he'll spark some idea in me."

"Come back whenever you're ready," Ward said.

"If Liho's guilty of two murders and a third attempt, he has to have a motive. Why would he do it, Ward? Blaine and Nona, I mean? What did Liho stand to gain by their deaths?"

"Nothing that I know of," Ward said. "Liho and Blaine were never friends, but Blaine was civil to everyone. Of course, I don't know Liho's relationship with Nona. But why does any murderer kill?" Ward talked as if to himself. "Psychologists say the motivation is either fear or greed, or both. I've suspected all along that Liho covets those

161

pineapple formulas. With Blaine out of the way . . ."

"But I know nothing of those experiments, Ward. I've no wealth, and Liho has no reason to fear me. An attempt on my life makes no sense. Delores evidently doesn't suspect Liho of murdering Blaine or she would have refused his help with Davao. I'm afraid for her, Ward."

"You think Liho may try to harm Delores? I disagree, Ginny. He's had ample opportunity if those were his plans."

"Perhaps he'll do her no physical harm. I think he intends to aggrandize his fortune by marrying her." I voiced the thought that had been festering inside me. "Delores is wealthy, and she's flinging herself at him. Surely you've noticed?"

"I've noticed. And you may be right, but I hope not." Ward stood, pulled me to my feet, and we strolled toward the villa like any couple who had just spent a pleasant afternoon on the beach.

For a moment I forgot the entangling web of intrigue that bound us. Ward's hand was warm against my own; I felt the throb of our pulses where our wrists touched. I wished that life could be lived in separated segments instead of in one flowing ribbon of events. If I could scissor this moment from memory of past pain and from fear of future misery — if I could perform this magic — I would be in love with Ward.

There in that isolated moment I saw only beauty around me, the hibiscus blossoms nestling in their green foliage, the tall pines forming a guard to shut out the rest of the world. I was alone with the most exciting man I'd ever met, and an inner glow bathed me.

My pleasant reverie disappeared as Hale Malani loomed on the hillside, the tilted corners of its pagoda roof forming a grinning mouth that mocked me. Ward was not offering me love, and had he been, I would have refused it.

Delores had returned from work and was sitting on the lanai so there was nothing to do but continue our game. Delores had no reason to view Ward as my protector, and I intended to give her none.

"Ginny! Don't tell me you've lured the composer from his piano." Delores grinned, and Ward spoke with more enthusiasm than I thought necessary.

"Right," he said. "Ginny sang her Lorelei song from a distant rock, and I ran to her side."

I felt my hand shaking in Ward's strong grip, and when I smiled at his attempt at humor, my face felt as if it might crack.

"What's the matter, Ginny?" Delores' face clouded with concern. "You look as if you might have had too much sun."

"I'm fine," I said. "All I need is a quick shower." I pulled my hand from Ward's grasp and hurried upstairs. Ward had tried to speak lightly, to make Delores think we had been enjoying a casual stroll on the beach, but I knew that for me our relationship had changed. Trouble has a way of uniting people, and I felt a oneness with Ward that surprised me.

CHAPTER THIRTEEN

I rested after my shower, and when I came downstairs, Pindora had supper ready. Delores seemed relaxed and quite willing to be waited on. She looked refreshed, and although she still wore a somber mourning dress, her green eyes sparkled with an alert awareness. Sweet-scented plumeria decorated the lanai table, but it was set for only two, and I spoke before thinking.

"Ward's eating alone?"

"Patience, Ginny." Delores darted me a conspirator's wink. "You've accomplished miracles. Never before have I known that man to seek the company of an eligible female. Don't scare him off."

Flattered that my sister considered me attractive enough to interest Ward Malani, I had a hard time disparaging her words.

"Oh, Dee! How foolish! For heaven's sake don't start playing matchmaker. I'm here for a vacation, remember?"

"Ginny! You're blushing! How becoming!

It brings out your eyes."

As we sat down, Delores faced the shimmering ocean, and I hoped that at last she was through staring at the gloomy mountain rain forest.

"How's work at the hospital, Dee?" I squeezed lime juice onto my avocado salad, hoping that my question would distract her from the painful subject of my relationship with Ward.

"I love my job, Ginny. Going to work has saved me from a slow death."

I was about to make some frivolous comment, but my sister's serious face stopped me.

"It's true, Ginny. I'd always thought of death as happening quickly, but now I know it's quite possible to lose one's life gradually, minute by minute, by clinging to the past and by failing to go on to the next experience. This hospital work has steered me back toward life. Yesterday Dr. Niilonu reduced my medication by half; I feel better already."

"Perhaps you'll cook your way back into paradise." I aimed for a light touch. "Years from now we'll probably be two elderly ladies basking away our lives in these sun-drenched tropics."

Delores smiled. "From the look in Ward Malani's eye, I'd guess that I may be basking alone, but I suppose worse things could happen."

When we finished eating, it was time for me to dress for work, and I was glad for an excuse to leave Delores. I wanted to say nothing that might throw her back into a depression, and it was all I could do to avoid voicing my fear and distrust of Liho and thus reveal our dependence on Ward for protection.

Then too I was eager to return to work, to be back in a position where I might discover some telltale evidence against Liho. Days were slipping by, and I wanted to see my way clear to remaining on Kauai.

Relieved that I'd outgrown my need for the mermaid costume, I slipped into a strapless sarong that Delores loaned me and admired the splashy blues and greens which were a perfect foil for my orange-red hair. Pindora had strung me a lei of pink plumeria, and the cool caress of the blossoms made me feel less bare on top.

Ward wore a brown orchid in his buttonhole, and as we got into the car, he tucked a matching blossom into my hair. He was silent during the ride to the Royal Poinciana, and I forced myself to remember that our afternoon's camaraderie had been strictly for show. Ward spoke only when we pulled into the parking lot.

"This's going to be tough, Ginny. You're bound to be thrown with Liho before the evening's over. Can you take it?"

"I hope so, Ward. I'd rather have him where I can see him. I worry when he's out of sight." I tried to sound matter-of-fact, but my voice shook. Ward walked around the car and opened my door, but before I could alight, he bent down to me and kissed my lips lightly, yet firmly.

The evening passed like a slow-motion film, painstakingly, minute by dreary minute. Dressed in hand-tailored slacks and shirt, Liho played the genial host and eased gracefully through the clusters of tourists as if interested in nothing more serious than giving them a royal Hawaiian welcome to the islands.

Although I recognized Ward's kiss as a continuation of our afternoon's pantomime, it, coupled with Liho's near presence, left me nervous. I scrambled the lyrics to two melodies and was verging on tears by intermission time.

Ward ordered black coffee for us both and guided me to an empty table beside a flickering patio torch. Fresh salt air blew in from the ocean and silvery stars twinkled through the poinciana branches as we watched Lelani conduct an audience-participation hula lesson. Like good-natured children the tourists responded to Lelani, to the tropic night, and to the flowing guitar melodies, but between dances I saw Liho and a pretty girl in a tangerine-colored shift weaving their way toward our table. It was too late to warn Ward or to make an exit so I forced my usual smile and a greeting.

"Dis is Missy Sharon." Showing off for his tourist, Liho laced heavy accents into his rumbling voice. Ward rose and introduced me, then without invitation, Liho pulled up two chairs and they joined us.

"Missy Sharon think her trip more bettah if she meets da missionary." Liho cocked his tawny head, stroked his dark beard, then fondled the ugly whale's tooth hanging from the chain around his neck. "Say something pious, Mr. Malani."

A crimson flush fanned Ward's cheeks, but he tossed the request back at Liho like a rubber ball. "My great-grandparents did come to the islands as missionaries, Sharon," Ward said. "But for real local color, you should talk to Liho. He's a full-blooded Hawaiian. Why, he might have been king of Kona."

"Is this true, Liho?" Sharon brushed a tendril of honey-colored hair from her cheek and gazed at Liho in wide-eyed innocence. Where were her parents? She appeared to be only sixteen or seventeen, and I felt sure there must be a chaperone nearby. But no one appeared, and Sharon's question launched Liho into a long story.

"Before da haole missionaries came to teach da Hawaiians a mo' bettah way of life, my people wallowed in sin." Despite his pidgin, Liho's voice dripped sarcasm, but Sharon didn't notice.

"My great-grandfather, he do nuttin' all day but play naked in da blue surf and golden sunshine. When he hungry, he eat sweet coconut, or ripe banana; when he tired he go to da grass shack to sleep. Then da haoles came bringing the joys of work and clothing, and disease weakened our race until it almost perished."

Liho unconsciously lapsed into proper English as his words grew more fervent. "The haoles dealt death and destruction, captured our islands, and have reigned in luxury ever since. The missionary descendants control the islands' wealth, the pineapple plantations, the cane fields, the sugar mills, while true Hawaiians eke out an existence as entertainers, tour guides, or beachboys."

Liho's tirade gushed like hot lava from the churning depths of a spewing volcano, and suddenly I began to comprehend the magnitude of his bitterness. He was sincere. In his mind he was a displaced monarch, and he saw the missionaries and their descendants as the instigators of his downfall.

Sharon's expression changed from admiration to self-conscious embarrassment, and I tried to rescue her.

"Sharon, have you seen the floral display in the lobby?" As I stood up, Ward nodded in approval. "Come, I'll show it to you." Sharon followed me as if hypnotized, and when we were away from Liho she tried to apologize.

"Miss Ardan, I'm so sorry. Liho seemed . . . I had no idea . . ."

"His bad manners aren't your fault, Sharon. I understand."

"But is it true?" Sharon asked. "Would Liho really have been a king if the missionaries had stayed away?"

"It's quite possible," I answered. "But if he were king, the islands would be quite different. Read some Hawaiian history before you condemn the missionaries, Sharon."

Sharon pretended to examine the sisal basket of orange bird-of-paradise blossoms interspersed with brown woodroses which dominated the lobby desk. "Liho's good looks almost blinded me to his rudeness. I should apologize to Mr. Malani."

"That's unnecessary, Sharon; Ward knows Liho." That was the understatement of the evening, but I could tell Sharon no more. She called for her room key, and I waited with her until she took an elevator upstairs.

By the time I returned to the lanai, Liho had disappeared. Ward was at the piano, and when he saw me he modulated into a saucy introduction to "Princess Poopooli," and amid a spattering of polite applause, I hurried to the mike and began singing.

After the terrace closed and we were on our way home, the air held the sweet scent of plumeria and a warm tropic dampness. Moonlight wrapped the surging ocean in a sheen of quicksilver, and I tried to forget Liho, tried to live in the beauty of the moment. Ward said nothing, and I matched his silence.

In the silky half-light of the moon the flagged terrace circling Hale Malani looked like a moat surrounding a dark Oriental castle, and as we approached the front lanai I again had the feeling that watching eyes scrutinized our arrival. Ward too must have sensed something unusual, because after parking the limousine, he followed me to my room, flipped on the light, and carefully searched the whole area including the outside balcony.

"Lock your door," Ward said, "and if you open the glass doors, be sure the grill is latched from the inside. If anything frightens you, raise a ruckus. Tomorrow, follow your usual routine, and I'll do likewise."

I found myself half afraid yet half wishing that Ward would kiss me goodnight, but he didn't: We had no audience. He left my room abruptly, but I knew he stood outside my door until he heard my key turn in the lock.

I wrote several pages in my journal before I went to bed. I really let myself go, and slowly I began to feel relief from pent-up misery. For years I thought I had examined all sides of my problems, but now I knew that I hadn't. Seeing things written down in black and white gave me a new perspective on my whole life. I thought less and less about myself and more and more about Delores.

After I slipped into bed I lay wide-awake for a long time. Even with the sliding glass doors closed, I heard the pounding surf, and the musky salt smell of the ocean was omnipresent. But it was thinking of Liho that blocked my sleep. His harangue about the missionaries had plumbed hidden depths of his dark personality. Had his bitterness goaded him to murder? I doubted that. Blaine had missionary ancestors, but not I. Nor Nona Ying. The picture was still like an incomplete line drawing, and I couldn't supply the missing strokes.

I was dozing when something, some small sound jerked me back to wakefulness. Was someone on the balcony? I listened intently for several minutes, but heard nothing. Rising from bed, I peeked outside, then, sliding the door, I crept along the balcony rail to the corner where I could see both front and side of the villa. No one was in sight, and I decided that I must have imagined the noises. Back in bed, I heard nothing but the pounding rhythm of the surf and the wind rustling through palm fronds.

I wakened at midmorning the next day after a dreamless sleep, and after slipping into swimsuit and robe, I went to the side terrace for breakfast.

Pindora perched on a chair to visit while I sipped coffee and nibbled at some fruit. Then with a flourish of her full skirt, she darted to the kitchen to finish her chores. I sat listening to Ward testing the same phrases over and over, trying different harmonies, cadences.

I wanted to return to my room, but instead I clung to Ward's advice to follow my usual routine. Dragging a bamboo chaise lounge into the partial shade of the balcony, I relaxed on it and closed my eyes.

When I heard Davao puttering at the water hydrant, I knew without looking at my watch that it was about time for Liho to arrive with instructions concerning the pineapples. Toting a fat coil of green plastic hose over each scrawny shoulder, Davao gave me the briefest of cavalier nods, then ignored me completely.

Since Delores had been working, she had been typing out instructions and sending them with Pindora to Liho's cottage early each morning. I was glad that her job prevented her from spending much time with her neighbor, but I wondered what Liho did with the instructions after Davao had followed them. There was nothing to keep him from copying them for his own personal use.

Of course Liho had no way of knowing experimental details that were completed before Blaine's death. He had no way of knowing these facts unless he had access to the wall safe. Respect for Ward compelled me to consider his theory that Liho was trying to steal the formulas, but nothing added up. Discrepancies flawed every theory I advanced.

Liho was coming. I tensed as he approached along the path through the frond-dappled shade. He moved with feline grace, and his brown tapa-print shirt, open to the navel, revealed supple muscles rippling under a broad expanse of skin.

Luckily I didn't have to speak to him. He followed a divergent path to the gardener's shack, and Davao joined him there. I was safe as long as Ward was nearby. I rubbed sweaty palms on my robe and forced myself to remain where I was.

I stared unseeing at yesterday's newspaper until I heard someone approaching. Fully expecting to see Liho, I relaxed when only Davao appeared. He was pushing a wheelbarrow filled with dirt, and I recalled Delores saying that he intended to fill the low places under the terrace flagstones. Not wanting to appear to oversee his work, I rose and headed for the kitchen.

Pindora looked up from her work just as we heard the crash. The floor trembled beneath us, and the first splintering of timbers was loud as a gunshot. The continuing rumble sounded as if the whole villa might be disintegrating. We rushed onto the terrace to see what had happened.

At first I didn't see Davao. The pungent odor of shattered wood and the smoky smell of creosote hung in the dusty air, and an upward glance revealed a jagged gaping hole in the balcony floor.

Severed tendrils of philodendron drooped like twisted, broken fingers where the heavy railing had ripped through the jungle-mass of vegetation. When I stepped closer to the debris, I saw Davao's crushed body under the splintered form of the amakua image. Both were sprawled on the chaise lounge where I had been reclining only moments before.

CHAPTER FOURTEEN

Frozen with terror, I stared until Pindora's wailing brought me to my senses. I tried to lead her away from the gory scene, but she shoved me aside as if I were a child in her way. I hadn't realized I was screaming until Ward sprinted around the corner of the balcony. Taking in the situation at a glance, he disappeared, and I heard the thud of his steps on the stairs as he hurried to us.

An orchid blossom dropped from the buttonhole of his khaki work shirt as he rushed toward Davao's body. Clearly there was nothing he could do to help the Filipino. Davao's head lolled at such a grotesque angle that even I knew his neck had been broken.

Pindora fought to pull away the debris that pinned her husband to the broken chaise lounge. Only Ward's sharp voice and firm grip persuaded her that her efforts were useless. Together Ward and I managed to get Pindora inside and give her a mild sedative. Ward called an ambulance.

"Shouldn't you call the police?" I asked.

"Police?" Pindora asked. "But it was an accident. Why you say police, Missy?"

Ward frowned at me. "Ginny's excited, Pindora. Of course we need no police. The doctor, the ambulance, they'll be here soon. You and Ginny stay inside. I'll see if there's anything I can do on the terrace."

Pindora and I sat in silence. She wept quietly and I could think of no words to comfort her. But I knew Davao had been murdered. And just as sure as I knew this, I also knew that I had been the intended victim.

With siren screaming Dr. Niilonu arrived in the ambulance before I had time to sort my thoughts. I heard sounds of debris being shoved aside, the low murmur of voices, then the slam of a car door. When Dr. Niilonu stepped inside the villa, deep lines etched sadness and an age-old weariness into his craggy face, and he broke the bad news to Pindora.

"He died instantly, Pindora. There was no suffering."

Pindora nodded. "For that I'm thankful."

"How did this happen, Ward? What caused it?"

"The timbers were rotted, Doctor," Ward said. "Termites. If the repairmen had come when I called . . ."

"I'm blaming no one, Ward." The doctor's

eyes narrowed. "But what really happened? Something must have triggered the crash."

"The wind, maybe," Pindora said in a hushed voice, "or perhaps it was destined in the stars that this was the time for disaster. Who knows?"

Who indeed! Ward must have sensed my fright because he assumed command. He ordered me to help Pindora pack some clothing while he telephoned her daughter in Lihue and then called Delores. Dr. Niilonu waited until Pindora was ready, then he took her in the ambulance with himself and Davao, promising to keep her in his care until her daughter called for her. I offered to go along, but Pindora said she preferred being alone with her family, and I knew Delores would be with her as soon as the ambulance reached the hospital.

When Ward and I were alone I spoke first and found my mouth cotton-dry, my voice reedy and brittle. "Shouldn't we call the police, Ward? How many accidents are people going to believe? Surely you know this last one was intended for me. Seconds before the crash I was lying on that lounge chair, and if Davao hadn't come to the lanai . . . He must have sat down to rest for a moment. Ward, I feel — responsible."

"Where's Liho?"

My voice rose in pitch and volume. "That's a good question. He was here earlier working with Davao in the pineapple bed, but I have no idea where he is now."

"Well, you can bet that wherever he is, he'll have a rock-solid alibi of some sort to cover these few minutes. You've no proof, Ginny. You didn't see him here, nor did anyone else. Any accusation would be premature; the police would dismiss it. Or even if they heeded it, they would never be able to connect the crime with Liho."

Ward rested a reassuring hand on my shoulder and forced me to meet his lancelike gaze. "Delores raised a hue and a cry that Blaine had been murdered, a charge she couldn't prove, a charge that made the Malanis appear ridiculous and that almost cost her her sanity. Spare us a repeat performance. I'm depending on you to be sensible, Ginny."

How had I ever considered Ward homely? He was strong and rugged, and his eyes had irresistible power. His nearness assuaged my terror and at least made it bearable.

"I can't stand much more, Ward, but I'll try to act sensibly. It's terrifying to know that someone's out to get you and that you don't even know why."

"Enough!" Ward frowned. "Let's clean up this mess. Think we can handle it? Work will be good for us both."

I nodded, Ward pulled the wheelbarrow into position, and we began heaping splintered balcony fragments onto it — like robots playing a macabre game of giant jackstraws. I hoped that hard physical labor would nullify my emotions. Although Davao had meant little to me, I churned with rage and fear. No one was safe in a world where such senseless killing could pass as accidental.

"I want this mess cleared away before Delores returns from the hospital," Ward said, "and when she arrives, I want you to treat this matter as calmly as possible."

"How can I be calm about death, Ward? Surely Delores will suspect foul play. Her mind's more alert now."

"You may be right, but we'll have to do our best to keep her thinking rationally, and cleaning up this mess is a step in the right direction. Pick up the big pieces first; we'll sweep later." Ward rolled the splintered remains of the badly damaged amakua image into the shade of a yellow-blossomed hibiscus, muttering something about repairing it so that his mother could still use it in her garden.

After a full hour's hard labor, the terrace was cleared, the blood splatters washed away, and the wheelbarrow replaced in its shed.

Only the gaping hole in the balcony floor remained as silent testimony to the tragedy. Ward and I relaxed on the front lanai, pulling our chairs well out from under the overhanging balcony and into the shade of the Golden Shower trees. My hair felt damp with perspiration, I could taste gritty dust in my mouth, and my hands were grimy and scratched, but I was too devastated with fatigue and fear to care about my appearance.

"You mustn't let Delores know that you suspect an attempt was made on your life." Ward spoke softly. "I doubt that she could cope with the idea of your being in danger."

"I know, Ward. I'm not sure I can cope with it myself."

"We've no proof that Liho shoved that image down, Ginny. How could he have managed it? Maybe the thing *was* pure accident. Perhaps we're seeing trouble when in reality none exists in this particular instance."

"Liho could have done it easily enough. I thought I heard footsteps on the balcony late last night, yet when I investigated, no one was there. Liho'd probably already done his evil chore. He'd probably already sabotaged the support beams."

"But no one saw him give it that final thrust," Ward said.

"Earlier, he went to the pineapple bed with

Davao, and he saw me lying in that chair. Davao returned to the lanai alone, but Liho easily could have headed home, then doubled back behind the Pandanus grove, climbed to the balcony on the carpenter's scaffolding on the other side of the villa, and shoved the image over the side without making a final check on his target. In the excitement following the crash, escape would have been easy."

"Perhaps so," Ward said, "but your evidence is circumstantial. Everyone around here knows that Hale Malani is termite ridden, that we've engaged carpenters to repair the damage. The crash has all the earmarks of an accident. By going to the police you would only put Liho on guard. We have to catch him, actually nab him in some subversive act before we dare alert the police."

"I suppose you're right," I said, "but I'm afraid."

"I wouldn't blame you if you caught the next flight to Honolulu," Ward said. "I had no idea that Liho would dare to strike right here on Malani grounds."

"I'll never leave without Delores," I said.

"From now on I'm your bodyguard, and I'm not letting you out of my sight. Think, Ginny! You must know something — something that makes you a threat to Liho or to his activities. Are you sure you've no idea what it might be?"

"Don't think I haven't tried to figure it out. But I know nothing that would make me of the slightest danger to Liho."

Although we expected Delores to call, the phone was silent, and at last Ward accompanied me upstairs and resumed his work at the piano. The thought of food knotted my stomach so I skipped lunch in favor of writing. My journal was almost up to date. With each page I wrote, it became easier for me to concentrate on the problems at hand rather than upon happenings of the past.

When Delores came home in the evening, I waited until she and Ward had had a chance to talk before I made my appearance. When I finally went downstairs Delores looked pale and drawn, but she was relaxing and sipping a drink and she seemed to have faced the tragedy with composure. Neither of us mentioned Davao, as if by ignoring unpleasantness it would go away. I knew from Delores' greeting that Ward had not told her that I had been lying on the chaise lounge only moments before Davao was crushed to death. And Ward was right. There was no point in needlessly alarming her.

The three of us forced down sandwiches and lingered on the terrace drinking coffee until it was time to dress for work at the hotel. I wanted Delores to go with us, but she didn't seem to mind being alone at the villa, and said that Dr. Niilonu had prescribed some medication and had suggested that she retire early. I felt that she was safe enough; I was the one in danger.

When Ward and I reached the Royal Poinciana, I was surprised and relieved to learn that Liho had taken the night off, and my lyrics rolled out more smoothly than they had on the previous evening. I wore a green and gold holomuu from the costume room, and at the end of the evening as I changed back into my own white dress I wondered why Liho had needed a free night. Then I remembered the Sea Carnival to take place the following afternoon. Perhaps he was resting up for the event.

After a silent drive back to the villa, Ward tried to soothe me. "Try to get some sleep, Ginny. Rest will help you more than anything I can think of."

"How can I ever sleep? I'll just lie there staring into space, staring and wondering when the next accident will happen."

"You can relax tonight. That bedroom's safe as a bank vault. The doors have strong locks. I'm a light sleeper, and I'll be near. Rap on the wall if anything frightens you, anything at all."

I took Ward's advice and locked myself in for the night. As I lay in the darkness listening to the wind moan under the eaves and to the surf pound on the shore, I drifted into a half sleep still trying to figure out answers to this crazy riddle, trying to plot some sensible action that would ensnare Liho and reveal him as the criminal both Ward and I believed him to be.

Although I was safely bolted inside my room, with Ward right next door, I slept fitfully, squirming and turning and glancing at my luminous watch dial at least every hour. It was the heavy, sickening smell of cigar smoke that warned me of a foreign presence, and I tapped lightly on the paneling that separated my room from Ward's just as a voice called my name in a hushed stage whisper.

CHAPTER FIFTEEN

Creeping from bed, I grabbed my robe, then slipped through the darkness, glad that I had had the foresight to draw the draperies across the grillwork that separated my room from the balcony. I unlocked my door to admit Ward, and we stood listening, waiting until someone hissed my name again.

In one swift motion Ward shielded my body with his and yanked the cord that opened the draperies. Bette Swanson stood inches from us, surprise transfixing her to the spot. Pallid moonlight glinted on her brassy hair until she shrank deeper into the shadow of the roof.

"Miss Swanson!" I fumbled at the lock on the grill. "Come inside. What are you doing here?"

The odor of cigarillo smoke permeated the room as Bette Swanson stood before us, looking mutely from my face to Ward's. I reached for the light switch, but Ward caught my hand. My teeth chattered in spite of the warm night, and I couldn't imagine what would drive this woman to my balcony at this hour.

"Whatever is troubling you, feel free to speak in front of Mr. Malani," I said. "Can I help you?"

"Only by leaving Kauai, Ginny."

Bette Swanson spoke my name as if we were close friends of long standing, and although I had always respected her, it was hard to remain in awe as she stood wringing her pudgy hands, a fire-tipped cigarillo dangling from her lips.

"Who sent you here?" Ward's voice was a hoarse whisper, but it projected a no-nonsense quality that demanded an answer.

"No one sent me. I come at great personal risk because — because Miss Ardan is my friend."

"You've met her once, or was it twice?" Ward asked. "And on the basis of those brief encounters you formed a friendship that permits you to intrude in the middle of the night?" Ward snorted through his nose, but I shook my head at him. Bette Swanson was pathetically sincere, and I wanted her feelings spared.

"Miss Swanson and I only met recently, Ward, but I've known and admired her for years through her records and performances."

"You needn't cover for me, Ginny," Bette Swanson said. "Our actual meetings were brief, but you treated me like a queen, not like a worn-out has-been. For that one reason I've risked much to come here. Please! Leave Kauai! You're in danger!"

Before Ward could reply, Bette Swanson slipped back onto the moonlit balcony. Of course we followed, but we watched in silent amazement as she eased her flaccid bulk down the carpenter's scaffolding like a trained acrobat. Bette Swanson disappeared into the dark shadows of the Norfolk pines that spiked the driveway, and we only saw a brief flash of her red muumuu as she disappeared onto the overgrown kapu trail that led back to her cottage.

"How do you suppose she's mixed up in all this, Ward?"

"Who could guess? But she obviously knows something. She may be in danger herself." Ward realized that more sleep this night was impossible, and he took my hand and led me downstairs to the spot on the front terrace farthest from Delores' room. Pulling two chairs close together under the branches of the Golden Shower tree, we sat down as if it were midday.

Bette Swanson had told me nothing I didn't already know, and while I found her nocturnal visit disturbing, it didn't throw me into another fit of terror. I was beginning to feel a peculiar detachment — to feel as if I were a spectator watching my own life from the safety of a great distance.

"Perhaps Liho is Bette Swanson's secret admirer, Ward, the man that Blaine hinted of to Delores. I suspected that she had a gentleman caller the afternoon I returned her scrapbooks, and it may have been he. That could be why she dislikes Delores. Perhaps she sees her as a rival for Liho's attentions."

"You're joking," Ward said. "Through his job Liho meets a great variety of beautiful women. What chance would Bette Swanson have to appeal to him? Why would Liho choose her? You may be able to see through her greasepaint veneer to a heart of pure gold, Ginny, but to be quite frank, most men would consider her revolting."

"I realize that anyone so immersed in self-pity is unattractive, Ward. But these are bad times for her. I prefer to remember when she was at the peak of her success."

"Your empathy and kindness compelled her to come here tonight," Ward said, "but we still don't know why. Do you want to take her advice? You're free to leave Kauai, you know."

"I'm staying," I said. "This land has

charmed and frightened me half to death, but I'm staying."

Ward reached over and covered my hand with his, and I felt as if it were a shield that would protect me from all danger.

"An island is many things," Ward said, "but mostly it's the dream inside the dreamer."

Ward and I sat for a long time listening to the trade winds and smelling the blossoms that swirled around us from the Golden Shower trees. Gradually the island yawned to life.

I was in love with Ward. I thought about my writing. I had set down the statement that I was a worthwhile person so often that I was actually beginning to believe it, beginning to like myself a little. Through the understanding that came as a result of my writing I could now face the painful scenes from childhood that still flashed in my mind from time to time.

I could see my father's empty place at the table and hear my mother lament that a man was interested only in his own pleasures. A few days ago my love for Ward and my ingrained distrust of all men would have clashed on the battlefield of my mind. Now I welcomed my feelings for Ward, but I was thankful that my thoughts were my own. I certainly wasn't ready to reveal them just yet.

The pink sky burst into a golden wash, and the sun glinted on the undulating ocean only minutes before I smelled the enticing aroma of coffee and bacon.

"Delores's up early," I said as casually as if I were accustomed to spending my predawn hours sitting on a moonlit lanai in a South Pacific archipelago. "Let's go say hello." As we entered the kitchen, Delores smiled at us from the sink where she stood halving papayas and spooning the dark seeds from the peach-colored flesh onto a paper towel.

"Good morning, you two," she called. "How about lending a hand?"

"What can we do?" I asked, glad to see Delores in good spirits.

"Ward, you pour the coffee, and Ginny, you set a breakfast table for the three of us out on the lanai." Delores had pulled the patio furniture as far away from the scene of yesterday's tragedy as possible and, as if by tacit agreement, no one mentioned Pindora or Davao.

"You two going to the water carnival today?" Delores seemed eager to link us together in as many ways as possible.

"How about it, Ginny?" Ward glanced at me. "Interested?"

The only thing I was really interested in was

getting some sleep, but I forced a smile. "Sure, why not? Are you going, Dee?"

"Have to work." Delores frowned, but the eager lilt in her voice belied her expression and puzzled me. She was delighted with her job, but she wouldn't have surprised me if she had asked for the day off in order to see Liho perform at the carnival.

Delores gulped her coffee, and Ward and I volunteered to clear away the breakfast things so she could get dressed for work. Before leaving the villa, Delores stopped at the kitchen and looked in where we were doing the dishes.

"Would you two irrigate the pineapple plants this morning? I've checked the instructions, and there're no chemicals or special treatments necessary today — just water."

"Count on us, Dee." I waved a sudsy hand.

Ward seemed ill at ease in the kitchen, and as soon as we put the dishes away, he suggested that we tend to the pineapples after we'd dressed. Here, I was the clumsy one. I man- aged to snarl the garden hose three times before we got it stretched from the spigot to the verdant pineapple beds.

Ward was soaking the second row of plants, and I was dreamily inhaling the pleasant, sweet-fruit fragrance that wafted around us when I tripped over the hose, raking it across the numbered pineapple specimens in the first row. To my dismay two of the plants came uprooted and lay askew in the red earth.

"Oh, Ward! Now I've done it!" I pointed. "I've probably jinxed the whole experiment."

Ward squatted to examine the two plants, then his gaze met mine. "You didn't do this, Ginny. Pineapple plants are tough-rooted; it'd take more than a graze with a plastic hose to upend them. Someone's recently transplanted these specimens." Ward stood up and absently wiped his earth-stained hands on his trousers.

"But why?" I examined the plant roots and had to agree with Ward that a mere tug of hose couldn't have dislodged them.

"Look, Ginny! These plants are different from the others. Compare them. The fruit's smaller; the leaf color's lighter."

I felt the roughness of the spiny, barrel-shaped fruit against my palm. "Someone's substituted these plants for specimens from the control group." I blurted the words, and Ward shushed me with a glance. "Is this the proof we need in order to go to the police about Liho?"

Ward shook his head. "We'll have to find the missing plants first, find them along with solid proof that Liho took them."

"I know where they might be," I said. "Oh,

Ward, I should have told you sooner, but so much has happened. And I wasn't, I'm still not really sure. But . . ."

"What are you talking about?" Ward asked. "Tell me!"

"That cave, Ward. I never mentioned it at the time, but when I swam inside that cavern I thought I saw a boat on the opposite side of the pool. What better place could anyone find to hide illegal activities? Especially anyone as crafty as Liho!"

"Why didn't you tell me this, Ginny? What did the boat look like? What color was it?"

"Ward! You'd hardly believe that I'd seen a cave, and with the tide blocking the entrance I could prove nothing. My first thought was that if what I saw was a boat, it might have belonged to Blaine. But I couldn't blurt out such an idea."

"Why not?"

"You'd have thought me a complete fool. Anyway, I may have imagined it; the lighting was poor. But even if there's no boat, that cave would serve as an excellent hiding place for anyone familiar with the ocean and tides, anyone with Liho's prowess in the water."

"You know, then, that Blaine's boat, the *Golden Dolphin*, is still missing?" Ward asked.

I nodded. "Delores told me. Ward! Let's quit guessing. Let's search that cave. We could take flashlights, lanterns, anything to help us see."

"No use going until low tide." Ward pulled out his billfold and consulted a tide chart. "That'll be this afternoon. But I agree with you. I'd bet the black keys off my piano that Liho has those plants in his possession."

"What good would they do him? Does he think he can start his own pineapple fields with only two plants?"

"We're going to have to act quickly," Ward said. "My guess is that Liho's trying to smuggle those plants off Kauai, to get them to private interests — maybe even in another country."

"Are the plants really that valuable?" I asked.

"It takes many months to raise a pineapple from sucker to fruit. Blaine's experiment dealt with shortening this time span as well as with producing larger fruit as the plants grow older. Liho would be low enough to black-market the formula to rival growers if they paid him enough."

"But could he smuggle information and plants off Kauai in a boat small enough to skin through that cave opening?"

"That has to be the answer," Ward said. "Liho's an expert when it comes to savvying tides and currents, and he knows the exact location of the breaks in the coral reef. He's skillful enough to take a small boat out beyond the breakers to rendezvous with a larger craft."

"How can we stop him?" I asked. "He's dangerous. Is there no way we could have him held for police questioning?"

"Not without alerting him to danger. Once he suspects there are bloodhounds on his trail, he'll cover his tracks and wait for a more auspicious moment."

I jumped as I felt icy water oozing around my bare toes. In our excitement we'd forgotten about the gushing hose, and we both stood with our rubber sandals mired in a sea of slippery red gumbo. I sloshed to the dry lawn, but Ward replanted the loose pineapples before joining me and washing our feet in the cold needle-spray from the hose.

"I'm going to Honolulu, Ward." Forgetting my fatigue, I wiped my wet feet in the cool green grass and headed back toward the villa. "It's still early. Is there a morning flight?"

"Wait a minute!" Ward narrowed his eyes. "Thought we were going to investigate a cave."

"I'll be back. You said we had to wait for low tide this afternoon. Liho'll be at the Surfer's Carnival all day. He'll be unable to enter the cave before tomorrow morning's low tide."

"I suppose that's right, but why the yen for Honolulu?"

"Liho surely has a criminal record somewhere, a record that we can show to the local police to persuade them to listen and to move quietly to help us. I'm sure we shouldn't tackle this alone."

"Honolulu's a huge city, Ginny. You'll get lost."

"I'll go to the surfing club. Delores brags that Liho's a former member, and he wears their medal. Club headquarters will almost certainly have some record of his past affiliations. Come with me, Ward. No one will miss us. Everybody'll be at the Surfer's Carnival."

I hadn't intended to invite Ward to come along; the words just slipped out unbidden, like beads sliding from a string. How ridiculous of me to fall for the first man who was kind to me. And that's all Ward's interest was — kindness. Kindness to a person who was suddenly deeply and hopelessly involved in his life. I was so engrossed in my thoughts that Ward spoke impatiently.

"I said I'd go along. You can't run off to Oahu alone."

CHAPTER SIXTEEN

Fearing that Delores might return home unexpectedly, Ward insisted on telling her that he had decided to spend the day in Honolulu with his mother. Delores' reaction was all that we had hoped for.

She suggested that I accompany Ward, spend the morning shopping and the afternoon sightseeing, then return to Kauai on a flight that would allow us to get to the Royal Poinciana in time for work.

Ward checked plane schedules, then called to me to "snap to" as he bounded up the stairs to his room. In moments the drone of his electric shaver announced that he was preparing to face the day.

My eyes burned from lack of sleep, and drawing the draperies against the sun's glare, I showered and dressed in cool, soothing dimness. My vivid flowered shift and green sling pumps seemed inappropriate for travel, yet I knew they would be less conspicuous than anything else I could wear. I wanted to give no one reason for remembering me today.

Arriving downstairs ahead of Ward, I wandered outside where the scaffolding still awaited the tardy carpenters. This side of the villa was still shrouded in shadows, and swarms of honeybees hovered around the green tangle of night-blooming cereus vines which were still studded with creamy chalicelike blossoms. I was so intent on the eerie beauty that I jumped as Ward spoke.

"Let's go. We'll have to hurry if we want to catch that jet."

I rechecked my purse for billfold and makeup, then slipped onto the front seat of the car beside Ward.

"This wild chase may be for nothing," Ward said. "Liho's smart and shrewd and he's probably accomplished at evading the law. Don't set your heart on learning too much."

I nodded, touched at Ward's attempt to protect me from myself. As we drove toward the airport, the splendor of the countryside around us defied description. But I felt as if a practiced hand had designed a beautiful facade to hide some hideous evil I could sense but never see.

A splatter of water pelted the windshield, and I thought it was raining until I saw a white spray shooting from an overhead irrigating system in the adjacent cane field.

"Ever see mangoes growing before?" Ward waved a hand toward a grove of tall stately trees which were loaded with round green fruit, a bit larger than apples.

I nodded, and Ward lapsed into silence as we passed a sugar plantation where field hands prepared for harvest. The air was smoky gray, heavy and sweet with the pungent scent of burning cane. Where the road hugged the shoreline, the surf churned into a brownish froth, tinted by topsoil eroding from the cane fields.

Tall shaggy eucalyptus trees growing on both sides of the road formed a green leafy archway overhead. After many miles of driving through cane fields, we arrived in Lihue and then raced to the airport. Ward parked the car, locked it, and queued up at the ticket window while I studied the gift displays in the brown thatch-roofed souvenir shops.

When Ward returned with our tickets, he carried a lavender vanda orchid lei which he placed around my neck and accompanied with a kiss. Flushing, I knew from his smile that he had interpreted my reaction all too correctly. We waited at our flight gate only a few minutes before being allowed to board the plane, and an Oriental stewardess with a yellow plumeria blossom tucked in her hair greeted us and showed us to our seats.

The fragrance of many leis overcame the odor of diesel exhaust, but as soon as we took off the inviting aroma of coffee overpowered both of these. Again the flight between these two neighboring islands allowed barely enough time to sip a cup of the boiling hot brew.

As we approached the Honolulu airstrip, our hostess pointed out Oahu's most salient feature, the jutting projection that was Diamond Head. Seconds later we had passed over Waikiki beach and I looked down onto Pearl Harbor whose many inlets stretched inland like pudgy blue fingers. Our touchdown was bumpy, but it smoothed out as we taxied to a stop. Stepping from the plane into the sunshine, I reached into my purse for dark glasses.

While Ward rented a Volkswagen, I found the address of the Honolulu Surfing Club in the telephone directory. With a red pen Ward traced a serpentine route on a green road map and then swung the car into a stream of traffic.

Ward's reticence vanished as he played tour guide, pointing out the Ala Moana district, Hickham Airfield, Fisherman's Wharf; but the fresh-fruit scent of the pineapple cannery distracted me, and exotic papaya and banana trees growing behind poinsettia hedges vied for my attention.

As we drove from the Waikiki area into the older part of the city, Ward pointed out the golden-caped statue commemorating Hawaii's famous King Kamehameha I, which stood across the street from Iolani Palace.

"Wish we had time to tour that building," Ward said. "It's used as our statehouse now, but it's the only royal palace in the nation, and the Malani family helped restore some of the rooms to look much as they did during the heyday of the monarchy."

"I'd love to see it," I said. "I wish this were a pleasure tour instead of . . ." My throat tightened as I remembered the grim nature of our trip. We rode in silence, and when Ward slowed the car I began searching for street names and numbers.

"There it is." Ward eased the car to the curbing and we alighted. A brown building, set farther back from the street than most, bore a yellow surfboard-shaped sign inscribed with the words HONOLULU SURFING CLUB. An imitation thatched roof overhung the plate glass front revealing a large muscular Hawaiian seated in a swivel chair behind a polished mahogany desk.

Ward held the door for me, and we stepped inside. The interior of the office was like a photo gallery. Glossy prints of smiling, brown-skinned surfers lined the walls, and across the rear of the room a trophy case housed silver and gold loving cups.

"Aloha." The Hawaiian's chair squeaked as he rose to greet us. "May I be of help?"

"We'd like some information about one of your former members, Mr. Liho Kalaka," Ward said. "He's appearing today at the Kauai Surfer's Carnival, and we'd like some pertinent background facts about his life."

I looked at Ward with ill-concealed pride. We'd discussed no approach to use once we found this club, and I admired his business-like manner which hinted that we were reporters at large.

"Liho Kalaka." The Hawaiian frowned. "The name's unfamiliar. Do you know what year or years he held membership here?"

Ward glanced at me through narrowed lids, frowned, and pretended to think. "When was it, Ginny?"

I gulped. How did he expect me to know the answer. "I'm unsure of the date, but he does wear that copper medal. Might that be a clue?"

"Copper medal?" Our host nodded. "Shaped like a surfboard?"

"That's right," I answered. "Do you remember him?"

The man stepped toward a bookshelf that flanked the trophy case. "We only awarded the copper medal during a five-year period." He pulled out a quintet of red leather-bound volumes. "Perhaps you can find your man listed in one of these yearbooks. There's an alphabetical index, and all the medal-winners are pictured."

The telephone rang, and the man excused himself, motioning us to help ourselves to the books. We looked through the volumes, but Liho's name was absent.

"He's such a phony, he probably stole the medal, or had one made in imitation of the real thing," Ward said.

"I doubt that, Ward. Liho's innate surfing ability is the one honest thing about him." I scrutinized the index again and paused with my finger under the name of Likeke Konapuno.

"Find something?" Ward squinted at the name.

"I suppose not, but the initials are identical. L.K. Let's take a look. If a person were going to use an alias, he just might pick one with his true initials. It would save trouble and explanations concerning monogrammed luggage and the like."

Flipping the pages to the picture of Likeke Konapuno, we both studied the likeness.

"This is just a kid," Ward said.

I glanced at the date on the page. "Ten years ago Liho would have been just a kid. Ward, there's a resemblance — the eyes, that feline, crouching stance. I'll copy this data. Here's his birthplace, his former address, and his school." I scrawled the information on the back of the tourist map, and as I printed the name, the letters pricked my brain like darts and evoked a memory I'd almost forgotten.

"Likeke Konapuno! Ward! I've got it! Come on, let's go!"

"What!" Ward replaced the books on their shelf, waved a salute of thanks to the Hawaiian, and followed me to the car.

In the privacy of the Volkswagen I explained. "I'd almost forgotten, Ward, but when I had Bette Swanson's scrapbooks, I saw this name on a clipping. Likeke Konapuno. I'm sure, because at the time I thought it strange that the marriage of a Hawaiian would interest a mainland opera star. Then later I saw Liho rip a clipping from one of the scrapbooks. He didn't know I was watching, and actually I had forgotten all about it until right now. But it was then that all these terrible things began happening, Ward."

"Slow down, Ginny. You lost me about ten sentences ago. What about this clipping? You mentioned a marriage."

"Yes, and that's what I still don't understand, but I'm sure this all fits together somehow. The clipping was a routine legal notice of a marriage license issued to Likeke Konapuno and an Elizabeth Timmons. Oh Ward! I thought I had something, but it makes little sense after all."

As I glanced at Ward he gave a low whistle. "Would it make more sense if you knew that Elizabeth Timmons and Bette Swanson are one and the same person?"

"Elizabeth Timmons is Bette Swanson?"

"Didn't Delores tell you that Bette is a divorcee?" Ward asked.

"She mentioned it, but I'd forgotten. Dee said Bette Swanson had been married to a Boston industrialist."

"The nickname figures, you know — Bette, Elizabeth. The islanders know her by her stage name, but I've had occasion to deliver some mail to her, and she receives correspondence under her married name, Elizabeth Timmons."

"I'm beginning to catch on, Ward. For some reason Bette Swanson and Liho are secretly married — and from what I know of Liho, that reason must be money." I rambled on thinking aloud. "Liho probably met Bette and sensed wealth, poured on the flattery to which she's most susceptible, and persuaded her into a clandestine marriage."

"But why a secret marriage?" Ward asked.

"For the money. Get it? Bette Swanson admitted that she never saved a cent of her own earnings, so she must be living on alimony. An eastern businessman might send payments for years and years before he or his lawyers learned of a civil marriage ceremony that took place in some remote Hawaiian village."

"That could explain Liho's high standard of living all right," Ward said. "The two of them certainly couldn't live in such a grand manner on Liho's salary."

"And that's why Liho's after me, Ward. He knew I must have seen the scrapbook clipping, and he was afraid this would happen — that someday I'd remember it and translate it into big trouble for him. Ward, we've got to hurry. How soon can we get back to Kauai?"

"Next flight's midafternoon. Why the rush?"

"Ward, we've underestimated Delores. Blaine's death was murder, and she knows it. No wonder she had to resort to tranquilizers! Blaine accidentally learned that Bette Swanson and Liho were more than good friends. He undoubtedly caught them in compromising circumstances, and Liho murdered him before he could figure out the significance of what he had seen."

"That's fairly wild reasoning," Ward said. "I'd like to go along with your theories, but . . ."

"But I know I'm right, Ward. Everything we've discovered today may take awhile to prove, but right or wrong we have to get to that cave before Liho does if we're going to end this intrigue. We have to get there before he suspects that we're onto his scheme, before he destroys any evidence he may have secreted in that cavern."

CHAPTER SEVENTEEN

Only after Ward proved with charts and timetables that we couldn't get back to the villa before low tide was I willing to consider what we'd do until flight time. Visiting the ancient volcanic crater that is now Punchbowl, a national military cemetery, or watching porpoises at Sea Life Park would have enthralled me under different circumstances, but today my thoughts were dark-plumed homing pigeons winging toward Kauai. At this minute Delores might be entertaining a murderer. I closed my eyes, unable to understand my sister's behavior toward Liho.

"How about stopping at the Banyon Terrace at the Moana?" Ward asked as we joined the surge of traffic flowing toward Waikiki.

"Okay with me, Ward. But will the hotel object?"

"No. The terrace is open to anyone." Ward parked the car beside the old white hotel, and I repaired my lipstick and tugged a comb through my hair before we crossed the main lobby to the lanai, where brightly colored patio tables polka-dotted the cool shade of a giant banyon tree. Its thick aerial roots grew like gnarled gray trunks from the low branches to the ground and gave the one tree the appearance of many.

Ward ordered guava-sherbert parfaits, but neither of us was hungry. The sweet-sharp flavor of the ice refreshed my mouth, but after a few bites, a bitter brown cord of fear wound around the base of my tongue until I couldn't speak. I watched the sun-hammered surf until a motley group of tourists gathered in the leaf-dappled shade of the banyon for a hula lesson.

Only half seeing, I watched the visitors try to mimic the fluid, supple motions of their pretty Hawaiian dance teacher.

"The hula used to be a solemn religious dance before it degenerated into a cheap form of entertainment for the whaling crews," Ward said.

"Oh, Ward! No lectures, please. Let's go on to the airport."

"Better try to relax, Ginny. We've a long wait before low tide, and the possibility that you saw a boat in that cave is remote. Even if you did, it's hardly logical to think that it's Blaine's."

"You still don't believe me, do you?" I asked.

"I'll reserve judgment for a few hours, but even if Blaine's boat is hidden in that cave, we'll still have to prove Liho put it there."

Ward was right. I was so sure in my own mind that Liho was guilty of horrendous crimes, that again I forgot about the lack of actual evidence. But first things first. I had to prove to Ward that there was a cave — and a boat.

"Maybe we should follow through on your original idea, Ginny. Perhaps we should check Likeke Konapuno's past, try to find criminal charges that would interest the Kauai police."

"That's useless now, Ward. We might find something, but we'd have to convince the Kauai police that Liho was using an alias. It would take too long, and it would warn Liho."

A blur of traffic swirled around us as we drove to the airport. I sat trancelike in the terminal waiting room while Ward checked in the car and cleared our flight tickets with the officials. My thoughts kept returning to Delores. How could she tolerate an egoistic, boastful man like Liho!

En route to Kauai I absentmindedly refused both the steaming black coffee and the golden pineapple juice that the hostess offered; and, smiling, she informed me that in case of an emergency I would find a paper bag in the pocket flap of the seat ahead of me.

Ward chuckled and adjusted my lei which had slipped down on the back of my neck. "You do look rather green, Ginny. If you've any dramatic ability, you'd better hope it rescues you before Delores sees you. Your face spells trouble as surely as if the letters were emblazoned like a crest across your forehead."

Ward's words were teasing and his lips were smiling, but I could see seriousness in his narrowed eyes. And he was right. I was going to have to cover my emotions, to find an armor. I wondered what else Ward saw when he looked at me. Had he guessed my feelings toward him?

Somewhere during the ride from Lihue airport to the mausoleum that was Hale Malani, I regained my outward composure, and when I saw Liho clad only in black swimming trunks lounging on the terrace with Delores, I forced my stage smile and called a pleasant greeting to them.

Liho didn't rise as we joined them. With his shaggy head resting on a crimson cushion, he followed my every move with watchful, glinting eyes. I shuddered and walked behind his chair toward Delores.

Delores' eyes were bright and her cheeks

flushed, and I wondered what she and Liho had been discussing, wondered if Delores had any idea that she was throwing herself at a married man — at Blaine's murderer.

"How was your day, Ginny?" Delores asked.

"Great," I replied truthfully. "Honolulu's a lovely city."

"And Ward, how is Mother Malani progressing with her decorating?"

"Amazingly well." Ward narrowed his eyelids as he gazed toward the ocean, then revealed information he must have gathered on his previous visit to Oahu. "She's dedicating the west room to the memory of Hawaiian nobility; she's using Pandanus floor mats, royal feather staves at the doorways, and brown tapa-cloth on the walls."

"I'd go for that." Liho spoke with lazy arrogance. "Sounds like my kind of room."

"How was the carnival?" I asked.

"Liho won first honors." Delores smiled at Liho and held up a gold loving cup.

Ward's voice was rough as sandpaper as he congratulated Liho, and although I wanted to shrill a warning to Delores, I mouthed a few polite words before excusing myself to go to my room. Once upstairs I locked my door, then relaxed in a warm tub of perfumed bubbles. The soothing heat and the pleasant fragrance gave me a feeling of euphoria, but when I stretched out on my bed I thought I could never sleep with danger so near.

Yet the next thing I knew I heard Ward tapping on my door and announcing dinner. In spite of my brief nap I felt like a piece of debris that had been battered by strong currents and washed in on a low tide, but I applied enough makeup to mask the ravages of fatigue and worry. I'd had a suspicion that Delores had invited Liho for dinner, and now as I returned to the lanai my worst fears were confirmed.

Liho had topped his black trunks with a vivid aloha shirt, and was pulling chairs up to the patio table. Delores had changed from her hospital uniform into a sunshine-yellow muumuu that set off her auburn hair and cameo complexion. Clearly, she was ready to enjoy the evening. Yet she stood with her knees stiffened, and although I recognized her familiar defiant stance I couldn't understand what she was steeling herself to defy. Me, perhaps?

Delores announced that Ward was having a tray in his room, and I wished I could join him; but it was too late. I was trapped. I saw the bright side of the situation; my presence prevented Delores and Liho from being a cozy twosome, but even that failed to cheer me. I couldn't play chaperone forever. Although food nauseated me, I ate as quickly as I could, complimented Delores on her lobster casserole, and excused myself on the pretext of resting before work.

When I came downstairs again, Ward accompanied me, and as we paused to tell Delores goodnight, her face was still blush-pink and her eyes glittered as they had years ago when she was a teenager in impulsive pursuit of some forbidden goal.

"I'll see you two later," she said. "I've been wanting to hear you sing, Ginny, and Liho's escorting me to the hotel tonight." The words hung there like a string of firecrackers — hissing, sizzling, ready to explode — but I smiled.

"Great, Dee! We'll look for you." I was elated that Delores was at last willing to make a public appearance, yet dismayed that she had chosen to make it with Liho Kalaka.

"Cheer up, Ginny," Ward said as we drove from the villa. "Being able to see them out in public is better than having to wonder what they're doing here at Hale Malani."

"I don't understand Delores, Ward. She's refused a dozen invitations to come along with us, yet she's all keyed-up about spending the evening with Liho. I'm worried about her."

"As long as she's unaware of Liho's secret marriage, she's safe," Ward said. "You're the one in jeopardy. Take care."

Illumined by flaming torch heads, the flamboyant poincianas cast their magic over the hotel grounds while silvery moonlight and soft trade winds charmed the carefree, unsuspecting visitors. That evil could exist in the midst of such beauty was incomprehensible, yet Liho's influence was like a creeping malignancy that threatened to overpower.

Delores and Liho appeared after intermission, and, stepping onto the terrace, Delores was a sensation. Heads turned, and guests watched in admiration as Liho gallantly held her chair for her. Delores' artless lack of makeup carried a certain natural appeal, and her leaf-green holomuu brought out the emerald tones in her eyes. Her pale petal-smooth skin pointed up a fragility that was in sharp contrast with Liho's rugged manliness. Even I had to admit that they were a handsome couple.

Somehow I got through the evening. Liho's watching, waiting gaze unnerved me, made me feel like a stalked animal, but Delores' smiles and applause gave me courage. Almost before the terrace lights dimmed to announce the close of the dancing area, Ward began packing away his equipment. Liho and Delores had already disappeared into the crowd. I glanced at my watch, hurried to change clothes, then ran to the car where Ward was already waiting.

"Where are they?" I glanced furtively into a dense, fern-tree thicket that flanked the parking area.

"They left ahead of us," Ward said, "but that doesn't mean they're going straight home. The Coco Palms stays open later than the Royal Poinciana; Liho could take Delores there for a final fling and also to give himself as much of an alibi for the evening as possible. He doesn't know we're on to him, you know. He has no special reason for hurrying."

"What are we going to do?"

"At the villa we'll change into swimsuits, leave our rooms dark so Delores'll think we're asleep, then go to the beach."

Luck was with us. We were first to arrive at Hale Malani, and Delores had left two patio torches glaring like orange beacons in the night. I followed Ward up the corkscrew spiral of stairs.

"Be quick, Ward. If they should come in before we've changed . . ." I ran to my room. I flung my dress across the bed, squirmed into my swimsuit, and jammed my feet into a pair of sneakers, but as I stepped into the hallway, a car stopped on the drive. I heard Liho's deep purring voice and Delores' silvery laughter.

"Quick! In here!" Ward closed my door, locked it, and pocketed the key. He pulled me into his room. "Can you make it down the scaffolding?"

"They'll see us — hear us."

"They'll sit on the patio for a while," Ward said. "Come on." He locked his bedroom door and eased onto the balcony, pulling me like a reluctant child behind him. Delores and Liho had strolled onto the side terrace. Ward and I seized our advantage and scrambled down the shaky scaffolding, then slunk into the black shadows of the pines. We spoke only when we were well onto the public pathway to the beach.

"Think you can find that cave entrance at night, Ginny?"

"I must. I know it's there, Ward, but if anyone sees us before we find it, we can always pretend that we're out for a romantic swim." I shuddered as I thought of casually swimming in the pool where Nona Ying had died.

Clasping the strong firm hand Ward offered, I led the way beyond the white beach and over the dark craggy mounds that marked the fringes of one of Kauai's inaccessible shorelines. The black rocks loomed forbidding in the night, although a fragment of moon bathed them in a fragile silver light.

Ward was more surefooted than I as we

blundered over tumbles of slippery lava boulders. The stench of rotting coral winnowed in the air like a fetid gas. Then suddenly the opening was there, across the gleaming waters of the cove. I gasped as I pointed at the black hole that loomed low in the side of the bluff. Sensing my reluctance, Ward led the way into the water. We swam across the quiet, protected cove, pausing only a moment at the cave entrance.

The interior of the cavern was a moist blotter soggy with inky blackness. Instinctively, we stopped where the moonglow cut off abruptly inside the cave mouth, and, treading the now icy water, I unconsciously eased closer to Ward, sensing unknown dangers lurking on all sides.

Suddenly my feet touched solid rock, and, scrambling onto a narrow submerged ledge, I stood waist-deep in water. Something swooped through the air. I stifled a scream as I felt wing tips graze my cheek.

Ward waited for a moment, listening intently, but now only the ominous living rush of water was audible. At last he risked using his waterproof flashlight, and as the yellow beam fanned an arc across the black opaque water, it illumined the form that I remembered. A small green outboard floated on the opposite side of the pool.

"Let's swim over and have a look." Ward jammed the glowing flashlight into the waistband of his trunks.

"I'm afraid." I held back and my teeth chattered. "This pool looks — abysmal."

"You're a strong swimmer," Ward said. "There's no more danger in sixty feet of water than in six. But wait here if you'd rather."

What a choice! I wondered if the narrow rim of rock on which we stood might extend all the way around the pool, if perhaps we could walk to the other side. But before I could suggest this, Ward eased into the water and silver-black ripples haloed his body as he swam toward the boat. If he could do it, so could I. I followed the weird light from his submerged flash and felt the icy water raise goose bumps on my skin.

Keeping my body as near the surface as possible, I swam a cautious sidestroke. I suspected that the pool might be bottomless; still, I had no desire to check its depth and perhaps put a foot down on some slimy, clinging ectoplasm.

Ward reached the other side of the pool, splashed onto the narrow ledge that did seem to ring this hidden chamber, and he thrust out a hand to help me. Rocks scraped my knees as I scrambled to the rim beside him. We waded to the boat which was moored by a rope to a jutting rock in the cavern wall.

"Is it — is it Blaine's?" Although I whispered, my words echoed as if I'd mouthed them into a microphone.

Ward jerked back a canvas tarp that covered the stern. "It's Blaine's." In the half-light Ward's face was an inscrutable mask as he peered at the outside of the small craft, then his flash beamed pools of light onto piles of lava rock that littered the boat's floor.

"Ballast," he replied to my unvoiced question. "Someone had to weight the boat deep into the water in order to get it through that opening. But it's seen no wreck, Ginny. This boat's been hidden here deliberately, carefully. And it's been repainted."

Ward flashed the light into the stern of the boat, and I gasped as the beam fell on a mound covered with a flame-orange shirt. A pineapple rolled onto the ballast rocks as Ward jerked at the garment, then held it up as if it were a foul thing that might contaminate him.

"That's Liho's, Ward! I'm sure. I saw him wear it the first night I came here." I told Ward of the strange incident on Bette Swanson's kapu trail, but he was intent on a more thorough search of the boat.

I shivered as the gloom grew thicker, then I

heard a noise that sent an icy wash of fear slipping over my skin. My eyes leaped to Ward's as the sound was repeated. Someone had coughed just outside the cave entrance.

CHAPTER EIGHTEEN

Terror-stricken, I grabbed Ward's hand as he flashed his light around the black cave wall which was jagged and corrugated with shallow, vertical ridges.

"Squeeze into one of those niches and keep quiet." Only Ward's equanimity plus his insistent tugging at my hand gave me the presence of mind to put one foot before the other and try to reach cover. The submerged ledge mercifully held us as we eased through the icy pool. Constant lapping of water covered our telltale splashes, and Ward risked no light; total blackness enveloped us.

Ward stopped inches ahead of me, placed my hand on a projecting edge of rock and ordered, "In there."

I crammed myself into the meager indentation and held my breath as I listened to Ward splashing to another crevice. Then all was quiet except for the sound of the sea.

Inhaling the musky odor of wet lava, I ran my shaking fingers over the clammy wall of this obscured niche. I might have been hiding in the jaws of a shark for all the comfort the nook offered. I wanted to whisper to Ward, to ask if he had found a concealed spot, but I didn't dare. A sixth sense warned me that an evil presence listened and waited — waited for us to give ourselves away.

I held my breath again, and as a crescendo of water sounds masked other noises, I strained my eyes in a vain effort to penetrate the blackness. Nearby something splashed into the pool, and although common sense told me that Ward must have loosened a rock, terror pounded me back into my niche. Silence. I groped with clawlike fingers in careful search of any pebbles that might dislodge and give us away. I found none, but just as I eased from the crevice a bit, I saw the light.

It was a beam from an underwater flash such as the one Ward carried, but here in the sooty blackness it glowed like a lighthouse beacon. Again I flattened myself against the clammy rock. The boat was to my left, the cave entrance to my right, but I didn't dare peek in either direction. As the darting beam raked the dark walls, I prayed that Ward had found a niche large enough to hide him completely.

The light wavered and dimmed, then I heard a splash followed by the cadence of a swimmer. I knew that our intruder was slicing through the black water. I risked peering around the protruding rock, and when the swimmer stepped onto the ledge where Ward and I had so recently stood, I wasn't surprised to recognize Liho.

A lump of fear blocked my throat as I watched him examine Blaine's boat. Would he remember exactly how he had left it? Ward and I had disarranged things as we searched the revealing contents of the craft, and Liho's arrival had startled us. Ward had thrown the tarp back over the stern. But the pineapple! The orange shirt! They were still lying where they had fallen when I dropped them in my fear and haste. Propping his flashlight on the bow of the boat, Liho flung back the tarp and peered into the outboard.

In the half-light I saw the muscles tighten in his thick brown neck, and as he leaned forward for a closer inspection, a pulse pounded on his temple. Hoisting himself into the craft, he picked up his orange shirt, gave it an angry shake, then bent to examine the exposed pineapple. Suddenly, crouching like a cat, he grabbed the flash and began slowly and systematically raking its beam over the cave walls. I squeezed back into my niche and tried to control my shaking.

Methodically, Liho played the light over

the wall opposite me and over a narrow ledge above the cave entrance, then he began the same probing search on my side of the cave. I could sense the impaling beam edging closer and closer. My mouth went dry and my feet felt as if they were frozen in chunks of ice. I wanted to disappear — to burrow straight into the lava rock, yet something in me craved to step screaming into the yellow glare of light, to give up, to end the suspense. I was about to give in when Ward shouted.

"Liho!" Just the one word. That was all he said. Liho darted the light toward the sound of Ward's voice, and I knew Ward had given himself up to protect me.

Weak and trembling with terror and cold, I clenched my teeth to keep from screaming. I forced myself to wait for what would happen next.

Ward was no physical match for Liho, but perhaps I could help in a struggle. At least the surprise element of my presence would be in our favor. Peeking into the gloom, I saw Ward caught in the beam of light.

"You!" Liho spat the word, then his usual arrogance returned. "You would have saved yourself much trouble by avoiding this place, Malani."

"Were you taking a trip tonight, Liho? In Blaine's boat? And did you plan to take your wife along?" Ward splashed along the submerged ledge toward the green boat.

If the questions surprised Liho, he didn't let on, but he reached into the waistband of his trunks and pulled out a plastic-wrapped object. Before Ward could reach him, Liho brandished a pistol, the barrel glinting blueblack in the flashlight's glow.

"Stay where you are," Liho ordered. "I'm no fool; I go armed where there is danger."

"Then you were expecting me?" Ward asked.

Liho shrugged. "Royalty has been in danger ever since your haole ancestors invaded the islands. It would have been more bettah for you if you'd stayed away from here, Mistah Ward. The Hawaiian in you lies dormant. You're snoopy. You should know by now what happens to snoopers."

Liho's words echoed in the dank chamber as if he were talking from the depths of a hidden tomb. I was terror-stricken, and thinking that perhaps Ward could catch Liho by surprise, I considered calling out to distract him. But the idea was ridiculous. Unarmed, Ward was helpless. But Ward refused to admit defeat. When I heard a subtle change in his tone, I knew he was stalling, pandering to Liho's inflated ego.

"Why did you kill Blaine, Liho? Surely you

knew you'd be caught."

"But I'm still free." Liho's voice dripped with a smirking arrogance that infuriated me. "And I'll get away with killing you too. Who do you think will ever come to this black hole to rescue you?"

"It is a clever hiding place," Ward said. "How did you find it?"

"Hawaiians always have found what they've needed on their islands," Liho said. "The ancient gods still rule; they protect their own."

"And most especially their royalty?" Ward's voice was admiring and resonant.

"Exactly correct. If the haoles hadn't interfered, hadn't cheated me of my heritage and forced me to be a gigolo, I would be a king today. I can't fight your powerful politicians, but I can still live like a monarch. The blue surf, the white beaches, the bright sunshine — they're free, and they're mine. Why, I even have a haole woman supporting me. Ward Malani, I live better than the great Kamehameha ever lived."

"But the pineapples, Liho," Ward said. "Where do they fit in? Surely a monarch is above working like a plantation hand."

I thought Liho would refuse to answer. Ward was leading him to reveal more than he should, but arrogance and egoism blinded him.

"I loathe pineapple, but I volunteered to help Delores in order to divert suspicion from myself in case anyone believed her accusations that Blaine had been murdered. With my lovely neighbor practically pitching both herself and her pineapples at me, I would have been a fool to have passed up my advantage. When I sell Blaine's experimental data, I'll be rich, maybe even rich enough to buy a divorce."

"Is that where you were going tonight?" Ward asked. "To sell information to your buyer?"

"No," Liho said. "Tonight I merely came here to check the boat, to make sure everything was in readiness. Tomorrow morning I get the last of the data, and I'll move on the next low tide."

As he said the word tide, Liho seemed to remember that the water at this very minute was rising. He stopped his braggadocio, maneuvered himself in the boat so he could keep his pistol trained on Ward, and at the same time peered toward the cave entrance.

"You!" He spat into the pool. "You try to keep me talking until the water blocks the entrance. You take me for a fool!"

"And is that the same mistake Nona Ying made?" Ward asked.

"Nona Ying." Liho paused. "A shame

about her. So beautiful. I hated to do it, but she, like you, was a snooper. She came prowling to Bette's cottage after dark with that crazy turban. Caught me where I shouldn't have. But you! You are the one who will die in this low tide!"

Liho laughed as he spoke, and before Ward could move, a shot rang out. I saw Ward lurch forward, hit his head on the sharp bow of the boat, then pitch into the black water.

CHAPTER NINETEEN

The boat drifted over the spot where Ward had disappeared, and I could see nothing. For a moment Liho fanned his light on the water, then dropping the flash onto the boat seat, he hurriedly rewrapped his pistol in plastic. Peering toward the cave entrance, he jammed his flashlight into his waistband then splashed into the pool.

Darkness enveloped me. I thought I would feel relief and release when Liho was gone, but when the sound of his splashing ceased, I experienced a terror that bordered on nausea and hysteria. Ward was dead. I was alone. And the tide was rising, rising.

I tried to scream, and although the sound came out only a rasping whisper, I continued until my throat was raw. Then I heard Ward's voice. At first I thought it was a part of this fiendish nightmare — this final burden, the hallucination that would deprive me of my sanity. But I croaked an answer and listened.

"Ginny. Gi-ginny." It was Ward. "Are you all right?"

Was I all right? A dead man asking if I was all right!

"Ward! Where are you?" I splashed through water and darkness toward the feeble sound of his voice.

"Help, Ginny . . . hurry!" Ward's cry faded, but I plunged into the pool and swam in what I hoped was the right direction until my hand banged against the hard, slick wood of the outboard.

"I'm coming, Ward. Where are you?" I was straining to see through the blackness when something rough and slippery snaked against my leg like a loathsome tendriled creature from the depths. I fought to free myself, but the thing coiled around my ankle and all but dragged me beneath the surface.

"Ward!" As I screamed and flailed the water, the sea retaliated by slapping a briny spray into my face.

"I'm holding to the line. Dive under . . . push . . . push me up . . ."

The rope! That's what tangled about my ankle, the mooring line. Relief gave me courage to free my ankle and follow Ward's labored instructions.

I got my bearings by feeling my way along the side of the boat, then bracing myself against the rocks of the wall, I gulped dank, musty air, jackknifed beneath the surface, and groped until I felt Ward's cold body touch mine. Deeper. I had to dive below him.

My lungs felt like overinflated balloons that might burst at any moment, but I fought my way down, down. Reaching upward, I made certain that Ward's legs were above me, then I reared toward the surface. Faltering under a strong downward pressure as he braced a foot on my shoulder, I struggled with renewed vigor, pushing his body up with mine. Again the wet, repugnant rope snared my legs, and, as though I had stumbled, I felt Ward's weight slip from my shoulder. I would have to dive again, but first I needed air.

Untangling my feet from the rope, I shot to the surface gasping and panting. Again I searched for the relative safety of the boat, and in my blundering I found Ward dangling precariously half in and half out of the craft.

Ward said nothing, but I heard his agonized breathing as he tried to pull himself to safety. "Hang on! Hang on, Ward! I'll pull you aboard." Standing on the rocky ledge, which was now deeply submerged by the rising tide, I grabbed the side of the boat and after a hard struggle, managed to hoist myself up and over. Slipping and falling over the ballast rocks, I picked myself up and groped with outstretched hands until I located Ward. He groaned at my touch, and nausea threatened me as I felt my hands grow damply warm and sticky with a substance that could only be blood.

I needed to know where Ward was hurt, but before I found breath to ask, he whispered, "Pull. Under arms."

I locked my hands under Ward's arms, braced my feet on the side of the boat, and heaved. Ward struggled to help himself, and together we managed to get him to a dubious safety.

"Hide, Ginny. Leave me . . . hide . . ."

Drained of all strength, I lay panting and exhausted for many moments before I remembered the flashlight. If only Ward still had it. I ran my hand lightly across his waist. Nothing. Then my foot struck cold metal, and I groped until I clutched the thin cylinder in shaking fingers.

I was unprepared for the appalling sight I saw when I flashed the light on Ward. He was covered with blood, and he lay with his eyes closed and his face as white as death. His hair was so matted with blood, that at first I thought he had a serious head injury. Then I saw his wound, a neat hole in his left upper arm. Gently I turned the arm and saw a terrible jagged tear on the underside where a freshet of crimson welled then trickled down to the palm of his hand. His position over the edge of the boat had placed his head directly under his bleeding arm.

Mercifully, Ward was unconscious. I tried to remember what fictional heroines did when their hero was shot, but thinking back over old TV movies that I'd watched I could recall little except glimpses of grim, sweaty-faced onlookers demanding boiling water.

There was no boiling water here, but I knew that the wound should be cleaned and the bleeding stopped. Was the bullet in or out? I wrestled with this problem only for a moment. There was little I could do no matter where the bullet was. If it was still in Ward's arm, it would just have to stay there until the doctor came.

The doctor! How absurd! Yet how natural a reflex to think of calling the doctor. I propped the flashlight so that the beam was aimed at Ward, then I cupped my hands and began dipping water onto his head and his face.

Salt water on an open wound? I didn't know. But it was brine or nothing. Thankful that Ward was unconscious, I bathed the injured arm as carefully as I could, and I thought, hopefully, that the bullet had gone in one side and out the other. The wound continued to bleed, and I ripped Liho's orange shirt into bandage strips and bound the arm.

Now there was nothing to do but wait. I tried to cover Ward with the tarp, but it was stiff and unwieldy, so I draped the remaining scraps of Liho's shirt over his icy feet then pressed close to him in order to share the meager warmth of my body. I snapped off the flashlight to save the battery.

I lay terrified and helpless in the darkness. I was exhausted from the exertions of the past hour, the past day. And to what avail? Liho would return, kill us both, and proceed with his plans.

Ward groaned, and when I touched his forehead, his skin felt feverish. I tried again to tuck the tarp around him, but its protection left much to be desired, and I molded my body to his, determined to warm him back to life. Like an uneasy watchdog, I dozed, wakened, then dozed again as the endless hours crept by.

I had no idea how long I slept, but when I finally awakened completely, I felt mentally refreshed although my muscles ached. The water was high in the cavern. From time to time I flicked the light toward the ceiling, and it seemed like days before I could detect that the tide was receding.

I had time to think, to appraise myself and

my situation. Ward's last words had urged me to hide, to escape, and I loved him all the more for them. But I had changed. I knew I had.

"You could change if you just wanted to." Again Delores' voice echoed to me from the past, but I knew she was wrong. A person couldn't change through desire alone. To change his actions a person first had to change his thinking, change his mental image of himself. My hours of writing had helped me do this. They had brought all the aspects of my life into better perspective.

For years I had nurtured my own misery, oblivious to the troubles of those around me. But in the course of putting my ideas and reactions down on paper, I began to open my mind and heart to others. I formed a new mental image of myself, and the change brought new direction to my life.

I discovered that my aversion to men was a result of my adolescent interpretation of a painful experience. When my father deserted us, I had placed the blame on some personal shortcoming rather than where it belonged, on some adult idiosyncracy. Writing down my reactions had showed me that I was at fault for letting an attitude assumed as a child influence my adult years.

Instinctively Delores had known this. The

same experience that had weakened me had somehow strengthened her. She had tried to set an example for me, for her older sister who should have been the strong one. That was why she had urged me to change my ways.

Now it was possible. For the first time in my life I didn't want to run. I loved Ward and I was no longer afraid to admit it. I wanted to stay here and to help Ward, and if I succeeded I knew I would also be helping Delores. I was through running. I was through cowering on the edge of a meaningful life.

Ward fretted in his deep sleep and fought off my hand as I tried to stroke his forehead, and my terror and despair gave way to anger. Ever since I had come to Kauai I had been full of fear and dread, of foreboding and pessimism, but now white-hot anger pulsed through my body. Ward might die.

I wanted to lash out at Liho Kalaka, to quash his childish, callow scheme. But I had no defense. The only weapon equal to a gun is another gun, and even if I had one, I wouldn't have known how to use it.

Suddenly it occurred to me that I did have one weapon against which Liho was almost powerless. Surprise. I had almost forgotten that Liho was unaware that I was in the cave; he had left feeling sure that if his bullet hadn't killed Ward the water would.

I remembered the oars lying casually in the bottom of the boat. Here was another weapon. Physically I was no match for Liho, but a surprise attack from above with a sturdy shaft of oak might give me the advantage I needed to escape the cave and dash for help.

I would as soon have dived into a pool of embalming fluid as into the cavern water, but I had to act. The tide was going out, and I saw a wisp of light at the cave entry.

Making Ward as comfortable as possible, I grabbed an oar and eased myself over the side of the boat. Half floating with the oar ahead of me, I sidestroked across the pool and groped with my feet for the submerged ledge.

From inside the cave entrance I squinted out into bright sunshine, then waited immobile for my eyes to adjust to the inky cave darkness. A strong swimmer might be able to dive through the lashing waves and currents that blocked the entryway, but in my weakened condition, I didn't dare try.

Now that a glimmer of light seeped into the cave, I was less afraid. By standing on tiptoe I managed to stash the oar on the ledge above the entryway, then I tackled the problem of hoisting myself up to join my weapon.

Although the bits of rock protruding from the cave wall were sharp and slippery, one toehold led to another. When I finally reached my chosen vantage point, I was completely winded. Now came the worst part of the ordeal: the waiting, endless waiting.

CHAPTER TWENTY

As the tide receded, a murky greenish pallor permeated the cavern, and again I could make out the outline of the boat floating on the far side of the pool. From my height I saw that the tarp hid Ward's body and I knew that even with the aid of a flashlight Liho wouldn't be able to see him. Anyway, I intended to give him no opportunity to look.

As I shifted my weight on the minuscule ledge, the lava rock gouged into my flesh until I found an endurable kneeling position. Bearing in mind Liho's left-handedness, I decided to take a practice swing at the approximate spot where I expected him to appear. I clutched the heavy oar with both hands, felt its slick hard smoothness in my shaky fingers. Then, balancing on my left knee and the sole of my right foot, I executed a brisk downward thrust. I practiced the motion again, and then once more.

What if I missed? What if I lost my balance and fell? I peered below and my stomach matched the churning action of the water. The ceaseless motion of the waves had a hypnotic quality, but I forced my eyes to the cave wall at the side of my narrow perch. After I whacked Liho I would have to move quickly, to flee from this ledge, to splash through the cave entrance to safety.

As the tide ebbed I inhaled the whispers of fresh salt air that rushed in from the cove. I breathed deeply trying to suck in courage to match my anger. The deep breaths calmed me momentarily, then I smelled another odor, a whiff of cigarette smoke. Liho was near! For a moment I froze in terror, then I remembered Ward and Delores, and all my anger and determination returned.

I held my breath as I saw Liho's shadow darken the sunlit arc of water below me. I clutched the oar, ready to attack the moment his head appeared — in that split instant when he was still crouched in the bent position necessary for entering the cave.

Liho's shadow wavered on the gold-green water like a black ghost, then his head appeared. As I lifted my oar to strike, a low moan echoed through the cave. Ward! Liho surely heard the sound too, yet he came forward. Every fiber in my body willed me to look toward the boat, toward Ward, but I fought the impulse, held my stance until Liho was inside the cave, then I crashed the oar down on his skull. He dropped under my first blow and floated face down in the water, his relaxed body grotesque and limp.

My only thought now was to flee from the ledge, from this cavern. Ward's moan had revealed his presence, and although I was relieved to know he was still alive, his cry only made my necessity for speed more urgent.

Unmindful of the rocks I scrambled from the ledge and floundered into the water. Flicking the brine from my stinging eyes, I spat out gritty sand and stumbled blindly toward the arc of light that meant freedom.

Splashing into the sunlight, I was resting a moment when I felt a hand jerk at my shoulder. My escape had been brief indeed; I wasn't surprised that Liho had revived and trapped me on the spot.

But it was Delores' voice that penetrated my anger.

"Ginny! Ginny!" She screamed in my ear, and strong hands braced me in an upright position. A tanned, uniformed stranger, wet to the waist, babbled at me in a mixture of English and Hawaiian.

"Ward!" I tried to shout, to tell them that Ward was in danger, but my words were like a carefully whispered secret. "Ward . . . inside."

The stranger released my shoulder, and

Delores led me from the water to dry rocks where we could sit. I was still in such a daze that I couldn't think. I could only see and feel and hear and smell, and I had a crazy sensation that the sun blazing on the damp sand smelled like a hot iron steaming a woolen shirt. Even my sensory preceptions seemed unreal, and it took a gigantic effort to organize my thoughts and to speak.

"How did you happen to come, Dee?"

"How did you happen to be here?" Delores asked. "And Ward? At first I was frantic when I found you were both missing, then I had the wild idea that you might have eloped."

I was too nonplussed to answer, and before I found my voice the stranger splashed across the cove half leading, half dragging Liho behind him through the water. I jumped up as familiar terror returned, then I saw that Delores' companion was a police officer and that Liho was handcuffed and offering no resistance.

"Found the papers right on him, Mrs. Malani." The officer wore a sheepish look as he held up a plastic-wrapped packet. "He was stealing information from you, all right. But we still have no proof that he murdered Mr. Blaine."

Liho sank onto the rocks, all his fight and arrogance gone.

"In the boat! Ward!" My voice shrilled as I realized the officer had been so intent on capturing Liho that he'd failed to see the outboard. "The *Golden Dolphin*'s inside the cave, and Ward's in it badly injured. Liho shot him and left him for dead."

As I spoke, Liho looked up, his eyes filled with a look of hatred and defiance, but he made no verbal defense.

"I can't leave this man unguarded, Mrs. Malani. I'll take him to the car and radio for help."

I came out of my stupor as I realized that Ward was still in danger. "That'll take too long," I said. "Ward needs help — a doctor. Right now! Why did you come here alone?"

"I merely answered a routine call, ma'am."

"After all the fuss I've made since Blaine's death, the police avoid my calls, Ginny. They probably flipped a dime to see who had to come out this afternoon."

"I'll take Liho to the car and call for help," the officer repeated. "It's the best I can do. I'll be quick." Delores and I nodded, and he shoved Liho ahead of him as he left us.

"We've got to get Ward out of that cave, Dee," I said. "I want him out here in the sunshine. I want him out of that tomb."

"Could we bring him out by ourselves, Ginny?"

"We can try." With Delores splashing behind me through the cove, we approached the cave entrance. "You wait here, Dee. I'll swim to Ward and row back, then you'll have to help me pull the boat through this small opening."

I tried to hide my aversion to reentering the cave; Delores was too weak a swimmer to accompany me, but I knew she would try if I showed the least reluctance. Before she could argue, I splashed into the dark water, waited until my eyes adjusted to the murky half-light, then grabbed the oar that had been my weapon. As I swam toward the boat, my strokes echoed hollowly in the cavern as if some spectre were imitating my every action.

Gaining the safety of the submerged ledge, I managed to loose the *Golden Dolphin* from its mooring. Ward lay motionless as my weight rocked the boat, and when I touched his forehead, the hot dryness of his feverish skin burned against my icy fingertips.

Clenching my teeth to stop their chattering, I dropped the oars in place and listened to the squeaking oarlocks. Delores was waiting at the cave entrance, and after covering Ward with the tarp to protect him from the salt spray, we tugged and pulled at the boat until we squeezed it through the narrow opening and into the shallows of the cove.

After what seemed like hours, an ambulance and a police car arrived. I hated to leave Ward, but Dr. Niilonu insisted that I would only be in the way, and he promised to call Hale Malani the moment he had information on Ward's condition.

Delores drove us home, but exhausted as I was, I couldn't sleep. I couldn't bear to lie down even to rest until I knew Ward was going to be all right. As soon as we bathed and changed into fresh clothing, we drove to the hospital, and during that seemingly endless ride we were at last able to tell each other just what had happened.

"Oh, Dee! You had Ward and me so worried. We thought you were falling for Liho. Why didn't you let us know you were suspicious of Liho? We could have worked together."

"That might have spoiled things, Ginny. Your playing the disapproving relative added authenticity to my act. But believe me, I never suspected that Liho would try to murder *you*. Nona Ying! Davao! How could he! I could think of no reason why he would consider you a threat to his scheme, and I actually believed that your fall was a freakish accident. Ginny! I cringe to think of the danger you faced. Why didn't you and Ward tell me *your* suspicions?

Why didn't you tell me what you learned in Honolulu — what you learned from the scrapbooks?"

I smiled. "We were afraid the shock might put you back on tranquilizers. Anyway, Ward was guarding me." As we entered the hospital, we met Dr. Niilonu in the hallway, and I knew by the way his craggy face broke into a grin that Ward was out of danger.

"A slight concussion and a badly ripped biceps," Dr. Niilonu explained quickly. "He passed out from loss of blood, but he'll be all right after a few days' rest."

"May we see him?" I asked.

"He's resting now, but one of you may step in for five minutes — no longer."

Delores excused herself on the pretext of checking on the next day's menus, and I followed Dr. Niilonu to Ward's room. Medicinal odors hung in the air, but I barely noticed them as I hurried to Ward's bedside. His dark hair curling against the white head bandage accented the sallowness of his face, but when I spoke, his eyelids fluttered and he groped for my hand.

During our ordeal in the cave and afterward, I'd thought of a million things that I wanted to tell Ward, but now they seemed unimportant. Neither of us spoke but in the eloquent silence I knew, from the warm pressure of his hand against mine, that Ward returned my love.

On the drive back to Hale Malani, I suddenly thought of Liho's legal wife. "Delores, has anyone broken all this terrible news to Bette Swanson?"

"The police have probably called on her, but I think I'll stop by and speak to her. No wonder she couldn't stand the sight of me! I had no idea she was labeling me the 'other woman'."

"Bette Swanson was foolish to allow Liho to sweet-talk her into a secret marriage, and she was dishonest to collect alimony that should have ended with her remarriage. Do you suppose she'll be arrested as Liho's accomplice?"

"Who knows?" Delores shrugged. "Surely she had nothing to do with Liho's plans. She did try to warn you, you know. I feel sorry for her, she's so, so finished."

"The first time I met her, I thought that too, but no longer, Dee. She's known struggle and defeat, but she's also had the thrill of reaching the top of her profession. Her life's been richer than most. And who knows? Now that she'll have to meet fines and pay debts, she'll be forced to support herself. She may become a great vocal instructor. I can't believe she had any part in the murders. She only thought she could buy Liho's admiration. She was a fool, but who's to say she's permanently defeated?"

"Look who's talking!" Delores laughed. "You! The gal who's going to spend the rest of her life singing ballads in a hotel bar and basking in the sunshine!" Delores braked the car in the driveway to Hale Malani, and, without giving me a chance to defend myself, she spoke again: "I'm going to walk down to Bette Swanson's cottage. Want to come?"

I shook my head. "I'll wait." Delores disappeared into the palms on the kapu trail, and I decided to walk on up to the villa.

The graceful pines formed a protective backdrop for the vibrant hibiscus hedge, and the cardinal blossoms danced as the gentle breeze cooled the countryside. Stepping around a bend in the lane, I looked up at Hale Malani and smiled.

I could now view the somber brown villa with its philodendron-covered balcony and tip-tilt roof as a friendly wayside retreat. Although I wanted to know Delores' home better, I remembered the touch of Ward's hand. His work here was finished, and I knew that when he left for the mainland, I would be at his side.

Never again would I allow inferiority feelings to shadow my life, to banish those people whom I truly loved. Of course, I knew I might have more of the old nightmares, but now I could face them.

The thought of leaving Kauai saddened me; but the future is a vision deep within me. Manhattan is a dreamer's island too.

The employees of Thorndike Press hope you have enjoyed this Large Print book. All our Large Print titles are designed for easy reading, and all our books are made to last. Other Thorndike Press Large Print books are available at your library, through selected bookstores, or directly from the publishers.

For more information about titles, please call:

(800) 223-1244

To share your comments, please write:

Publisher
Thorndike Press
295 Kennedy Memorial Drive
Waterville, ME 04901